MONTANA MAVERICKS

Welcome to Big Sky Country. Where free-spirited men and women discover love on the range.

MONTANA MAVERICKS: BEHIND CLOSED DOORS

Shhh! Can you keep a secret?
The mayor has resigned and the town is in a tizzy. From fake romances to clandestine crushes, nothing in Tenacity as it seems. The only thing these cowboys know for sure is this: They need the love of a good woman to make things right!

Sage Abernathy has come back to town after fifteen years with not just one secret, but two. The fact that she still harbors feelings for the ex-mayor's son, Brent Woodson, probably wouldn't shock anyone. But her second secret involves the scandal that rocked Brent's family all those years ago. If she reveals now what she knew then, she could lose what she longs for most: a second chance with her first love...

Dear Reader,

Rancher Brent Woodson used to be one of the most eligible bachelors in Tenacity, Montana—until his family's shocking secrets were exposed. With his reputation unfairly destroyed, half the town thinks he's no good, while half reserves judgment as he works to restore his name and reputation.

When an old flame returns to town, Brent figures that Sage Abernathy won't want anything to do with him. He didn't deserve her fifteen years ago, and he certainly doesn't now. To his surprise, they quickly rekindle their romance, and her belief in him means everything to him. But Sage is keeping an explosive secret that threatens more than just their own future.

I hope you enjoy Brent and Sage's story! I love to hear from readers, so feel free to reach out to me (contact info at my website: MelissaSenate.com) and friend me/follow on various social media.

Warmest regards,

Melissa Senate

THE MAVERICK'S
DO-OVER

MELISSA SENATE

MONTANA MAVERICKS

Special thanks and acknowledgment are given to Melissa Senate for her contribution to the Montana Mavericks: Behind Closed Doors miniseries.

MONTANA MAVERICKS

MIX
Paper | Supporting responsible forestry
FSC® C021394
www.fsc.org

PLEASE RECYCLE
THIS PRODUCT IS RECYCLABLE

Recycling programs for this product may not exist in your area.

ISBN-13: 978-1-335-54086-7

The Maverick's Do-Over

Harlequin Enterprises ULC
22 Adelaide St. West, 41st Floor
Toronto, Ontario M5H 4E3, Canada
www.Harlequin.com

HarperCollins Publishers
Macken House, 39/40 Mayor Street Upper,
Dublin 1, D01 C9W8, Ireland
www.HarperCollins.com

Printed in Lithuania

Melissa Senate has written many novels for Harlequin and other publishers, including her debut, *See Jane Date*, which was made into a TV movie. She also wrote seven books for Harlequin Special Edition under the pen name Meg Maxwell. Her novels have been published in over twenty-five countries. Melissa lives on the coast of Maine with her son; their rescue shepherd mix, Flash; and a lap cat named Cleo. For more information, please visit her website, melissasenate.com.

Visit the Author Profile page at Harlequin.com for more titles.

In loving memory of my mother.

Chapter One

"You're the *worst*, Brent Woodson."

Brent Woodson winced and kept his head down as he made his way through the big crowd in Tenacity Park, not wanting to know who'd hurled the insult at him. Seemed like the entire town had come out this morning for the inauguration of the new mayor. With Brent's name still mud among some people and his reputation not quite out of the gutter, any number of Tenacity, Montana's residents could have muttered those words.

Until six months ago, Brent had been the closest thing to town royalty in Tenacity. From a good family—supposedly. Son of the—then—mayor. Remembered as the high school football star when winning games and making it to championships boosted morale and made folks believe anything was possible in the hardscrabble town. A successful rancher. Lots of friends and one of Tenacity's most eligible bachelors at thirty-one.

Now, despite Brent's efforts at trying to show the town who he was, most women wouldn't dare date Brent if they cared about what people thought. He could count his friends on one hand—and that included his sister.

In this strange new world Brent found himself in, one of those friends—who until six months ago was Brent's sworn enemy and the biggest reason why folks hated his guts—walked beside him.

"Ignore them," Barrett Deroy said, clapping him on the shoulder as they headed toward the festooned stage set up in the center of the park for the event. "You know who you are. That's all that matters. Trust me, I should *know*. I was in your shoes for fifteen years. My *own mother* believed the worst about me."

Brent winced again. Barrett had gone through hell— and it was all Brent's family's fault. Fifteen years ago, *a lot* of money had been stolen from the town's coffers. Some of that money had been earmarked for much-needed revitalization efforts, so the theft had been a double blow. When the Deroy family, including six-teen-year-old Barrett, fled in the middle of the night, gossip spread fast that he'd taken the money and the Deroys disappeared to avoid prosecution. No one had been able to track them down, so everyone figured they'd changed their names. As the town's economy suffered from the deficit in funds, the Deroy name was held in deep contempt.

But then Barrett returned to town, determined to clear that name, particularly his. Thanks to a deep dive into the past, including a ninetysomething psychic, the truth had come out. The money, down to the penny, was found buried under a boulder on property the *Woodson* family used to own, along with a strange note: *You've got the wrong man.* Folks had taken that to mean Barrett was that wrong man—and that Brent's dad or possibly Brent himself had been the thief and spread gossip to frame Barrett. Brent's motive? His big crush on the girl who liked Barrett instead. Competition gone.

Nope. In fact, the real story was worse. To the point that it still turned Brent's stomach.

Brent's mother, June Woodson, and Barrett's father, Barrett Deroy Sr., had been having an affair. Right under everyone's nose. And it had been Brent's *mother* who'd stolen the money—so that she and her lover could run away together. Brent's father had found out and concocted a secret plan: He went to Deroy Sr. and blackmailed him. If the Deroys didn't leave town, Clifford Woodson, a respected businessman, would frame Barrett for the theft *and* tell Mrs. Deroy about the affair. If they did leave, Clifford wouldn't say a word, and the family could just move on and start over—far away from Tenacity.

And so the Deroys left and gossip did its job for Clifford Woodson. Everyone believed Barrett Jr., just sixteen, stole the money. Brent's mother didn't know that her husband had gone to her lover behind her back. Didn't know why the man she planned to run away with had run away without her—and with his family instead.

In their absence, the Deroys had become the talk of the town for a while. How they were "trash" with a teenage thief for a son. How they disappeared in the night with the town's hopes for change. But then Nina Sanchez, Barrett's girlfriend back then, asked her great-uncle Stanley, an amateur sleuth, and his psychic wife, Winona, to try to find out what had become of the Deroys. Of Barrett, whom she'd never forgotten.

And now, Nina and Barrett were engaged. Everyone knew the whole sordid, sorry story, all the details.

Well, except a few. There were questions about the money—like why June Woodson hadn't returned it after the Deroys left. She could have done that on the down-low, right? But she hadn't. Instead, she'd let thousands of dollars stay buried on the property where the Woodsons had lived back then. They'd long since moved to a big house in town. At least the town had gotten the money back once the new owners of the property learned they didn't get to keep it, after all. The funds were back in the town coffers.

Then there was the question of retribution. Justice. But because of the statute of limitations in Montana, time had run out on prosecuting anyone for anything, and so the Woodsons and Barrett Sr. had stayed mum. Mrs. Deroy had kept quiet for years because she'd thought her teenage son was a thief and wanted to protect him. She'd been afraid of the truth then, and she was still afraid. Like everyone involved. There were little things that didn't make sense, but no answers were forthcoming, no matter how often Brent asked his parents, and at this point, people just wanted to forget the whole thing.

Brent couldn't, though. First of all, no one would let him, and secondly, he didn't feel his family deserved a lick of grace. Except his sister, Victoria. She'd been just twelve years old back then, and for her sake, he wished for a do-over. A new slate, if not a perfectly clean one. A second chance.

The problem was that very few people believed that Brent hadn't known what his family had done. That he hadn't just stayed quiet to protect them. But he hadn't known. It had taken a while and some very tense talks with Barrett, but last summer the guy had come to believe that Brent was being honest. Brent could never put into words the relief he'd felt at that.

That Barrett had forgiven Brent and believed him, believed *in* him, meant more to Brent than he could ever express. Brent Woodson hadn't exactly been kind to Barrett when he'd first come back to town. Crazy thing was, Brent hadn't even realized what a privileged jerk he'd been his entire life until Barrett's return— and the truth had made itself known about what Brent's mother and father had each done. He understood why his name was mud. But Barrett had extended a hand to Brent and had invited him to work with him on the foundation he'd been starting up to revitalize Tenacity. Both of them now focused on the town's future rather than on their past. It had been exactly what the two had needed.

Be more like Barrett had practically become his mantra.

He gave Barrett a clap back. "I know who I am," Brent repeated hesitantly, hoping it would stick. He *didn't* know who he was—not yet, anyway. Overnight, the truth, and the realization that he'd been that privileged jerk, had turned him into a completely new person—humbled, sorry, determined to do better. Be better. Now, Brent Woodson was still getting to know who he was now—a man who'd been blind to a lot. A man who had to come to terms with the fact that he'd never have a good relationship with his parents again. A man who understood why folks in Tenacity thought he was a lying scumbucket.

"How do you do it?" Brent asked Barrett as they headed up the back steps to the stage. The two of them would be speaking after the inauguration about their foundation and its plans to revitalize Tenacity with a very exciting venture. They took their places behind where the soon-to-be mayor and her children were huddled with smiles and excited chatter. "How do you manage to stay so calm, cool, and forgiving after everything you and your family were put through?" Brent asked.

Barrett gave a casual shrug, but Brent knew the guy now, much better than he had when they were in school together, vying for the same girl. Barrett Deroy was strong, solid, and absolutely knew who he was. These days, he was Brent's role model. He shook his head at the irony. "Look, life is good," Barrett said. "Very good. So I'd rather focus on the here and now." He craned his neck to look out at the crowd at the front of the stage, and Brent could easily see who his friend was looking at. Barrett's fiancée, Nina Sanchez, stood there in the second row, smiling at him in encouragement. "And trust me, the right woman can make anything better."

Brent nodded. He'd once thought Nina Sanchez was his *own* right woman. But that was fifteen years ago, when Brent had believed his own hype. Of course Nina had chosen Barrett over him. Because Barrett had been true blue. Back then, Brent had been a legend in his own mind.

So much so that he'd barely noticed the girl he'd been seeing at the time—Sage Abernathy. A summer fling, a rebound romance for Brent. They'd barely kissed because Sage had been a year younger and had never dated a boy until him. She was smart and funny and kind and full of interesting stories, but he'd barely paid attention to her because he'd had a huge crush Barrett's girl. He shook his head at how dumb he'd been. He'd blown it with Sage, who'd been right there. Who'd probably had serious feelings for him.

Barrett had helped Brent believed that he had a second chance in Tenacity. That he could repair his standing, his reputation. But the way Brent had treated Sage back then, he'd never have a second chance with *her*. This was all ancient history, of course, so the chance he'd really want was to apologize.

If Brent had a chance to see Sage again, he'd let her know he had regrets for how he'd treated her. But she and her family had moved far away just a few months into their romance, and that had been that.

Brent looked out into the crowd. There had to be hundreds of people here. No surprise, given that Tenacity was not only swearing in a new mayor after all the recent unrest, but JenniLynn Garrett would be the town's first female mayor in a generation. And today was January 1. New year, new beginning. Everyone was excited for the changes coming. JenniLynn would be discussing her plans for the town, and then she'd turn the mic over to Barrett and Brent to discuss their foundation.

"I hope I don't choke with everyone staring at me when it's my turn to speak," Brent whispered to Barrett, his heart starting to beat a little too fast. Looking at the crowd, he could see people giving him the side-eye, whispering while glaring at him. "I won't be surprised if someone throws a half-eaten breakfast sandwich at my head. Or flings a cup of coffee at me. Maybe even a dog-poop bag—an open one."

Barrett raised an eyebrow. "Hey, no worries—they won't risk hitting me with that instead. Not after I got back my good name." He chuckled, then sobered up fast. "Brent, you've *got* this. *We've* got this. When it's our turn to talk, just focus on why we're here, and forget everything else. Like the past. Your family. My family. Everyone. Just remember why we're here and how we're going to help revitalize Tenacity. That'll help people see the real Brent Woodson."

"Good advice," Brent said, letting out a breath. He lifted his Stetson, running a hand through his hair. Barrett was right. This *was* his second chance—and he truly cared so much about Tenacity. The foundation was their way of giving back where their families had taken away. This was a big deal for both of them.

"What's that lying cheat doing up there?"

Brent winced again at the mutter from the front row. He'd think he'd be used to it by now. But the insults, the side-eyes, the glares and whispers still hurt. Hard.

"Ignore, ignore, ignore," Barrett whispered. "Plenty

of people want to hear from you, Brent. The truth is the truth, and it always outs. You were as clueless about what your family did—what *my* family did—as I was. Sometimes it takes a while, but you're a good guy and you're here for the town. So ignore the jerks spewing bile."

Thank God for Barrett.

Brent couldn't stop wondering how he *had* been so clueless, though. To the point that he understood why almost everyone seemed to believe he'd been complicit in his parents' dirty deeds—or had known about them and stayed quiet. Sure, he'd been well aware that his dad, the once-esteemed Mayor Clifford Woodson, had the heart and soul of a politician, but he never imagined that his father was unethical, let alone a criminal with no conscience. Brent hadn't spoken to his father in a couple of months now. And he still didn't know what to make of his mother, June, whose own actions helped set off the terrible chain of events that led to Barrett's family's downfall. Heck, Tenacity's downfall—and a family's banishment.

As the town clerk stepped up the microphone at the podium to start the festivities, Brent reminded himself that Barrett Deroy had been through much worse than Brent had. *Perspective*, Brent told himself. *Barrett lost fifteen years to whispers and lies and people thinking the worst of him and his family. All because of the Woodsons. You've been dealing with fall-out for six months and have that second chance. So do like Barrett just said and forget the past for right now. Focus on the speech you'll give.*

Today held a lot of promise for Brent. Even if the event itself—the mayoral inauguration—reminded him of exactly who his father was and that there were shady people hiding in plain sight. Hopefully now, all that was over. After Brent's disgraced father had to step down as mayor last summer, the town's fraudulently elected acting mayor, Marty Moore, had had to step down too. Brent was pretty sure his father had played a part in the ballot-tampering to get Marty elected back in November so that Clifford Woodson's future might not be as grim. That was yet to be decided. When their ballot-tampering scheme was discovered, and a recount deemed JenniLynn Garrett the rightful winner, it came out that her own selfish, self-serving husband had worked in cahoots with Marty to get him elected—and now she was taking on running the town as a single mother of three young daughters and going through a divorce. Everyone was in her corner. Cliff, Marty, and JenniLynn's soon-to-be ex-husband, Rob, denied wrongdoing, lying through their veneered teeth.

Brent was so damned tired of liars.

Now, as JenniLynn Garrett was sworn in and officially became Tenacity's new mayor, vowing to uphold the duties of the office—unlike the past two mayors—the crowd cheered and wolf-whistled. Mayor Garrett promised to work with everyone to rebuild Tenacity. The more she spoke about her plans, the more excited the crowd grew. Brent too. And suddenly it was his and Barrett's turn to speak about their foundation's very exciting plans for a dinosaur park that would bring much revenue and fanfare to Tenacity, putting the small, scrappy town on the map.

As Barrett wrapped up his portion of the talk, Brent could see the respect and admiration on the people's faces. He wondered if he'd ever be well-thought-of again in Tenacity. Now that Barrett was introducing him, as if Brent needed any introduction, he didn't see open, accepting faces. And he could hear were the whispers.

As Brent moved over to the podium and the mic, his gaze landed on Barrett's fiancée. Nina was mouthing something to Barrett—*You were great*, Brent was pretty sure he'd lip-read. He wished he had his own special support system in the crowd. Yeah, his sister was somewhere among all those people—she'd been so young when everything had happened, so she'd thankfully escaped public scorn when the truth came out. But he wished he had a significant other to cheer him on this morning. Maybe now, with his more public role with the foundation and the town revitalization, he'd earn back trust—and his love life might improve. That would be nice.

Maybe one day he'd fall in love again. He'd hadn't since high school, since Nina. He was completely over his first—and completely unrequited—love, and wished her and Barrett all the happiness in the world. A few times in his twenties he'd thought he was in love, but then the feelings faded once he got to know the woman behind the very pretty face and hot body, which had been his main interest. He shook his head at himself now for being so shallow.

Sage Abernathy's face floated into his mind, though she'd be fifteen years older now. Thirty. And probably married, maybe with children. He recalled that she wanted two or three. He remembered how she'd looked at him, as if he hung the moon, and regretted having been too cocky, too arrogant to be careful with her tender feelings.

He'd thought about Sage plenty over the years. In fact, thinking about her now, the way she'd looked at him, seemed to think so highly of him, buoyed him right through his speech. Gave him a boost of confidence, of belief in himself.

He was wrapping up his talk when he froze for a second, luckily at the end of a sentence.

Was he seeing things, or was Sage Abernathy actually standing in the third row?

He peered more closely at her and almost gasped. Those soft brown eyes, the sweetness in her expression, the one dimple in her right cheek, the long blond wavy hair. Her favorite color—red—in her wool peacoat and plaid scarf. The jeans and brown cowboy boots she'd worn even in summer. The tall, slender physique. It *was* her.

And she was looking right at him.

Her expression was unreadable. What was she thinking? How long had she been back in Tenacity? Did she know about his family's problems? His?

Who was he kidding? He was sure someone had filled her in, if she hadn't heard the gossip within minutes of arriving back in town.

He had no doubt what she was thinking. *I sure dodged a bullet.*

* * *

For fifteen long years now, Sage Abernathy had wondered how she'd feel if she saw her first love again. If she'd still think Brent Woodson was the best-looking guy she'd ever seen. If she'd get butterflies in her stomach. If her heart would speed up. If just being near him would make her forget all the things in her life that were bothering her. And a lot had been bothering her—then and now.

Yes to all. She'd been just fifteen years old when she'd unexpectedly come across Brent in this very park at the start of summer. He'd been sitting by himself on a bench at dusk, staring at the ducks in the pond and looking kind of miserable. She'd been crossing through the park on her way home from a friend's house and dared to ask him if he was okay. He hadn't even looked up. So she asked again, and then he finally seemed to hear her. He'd said, *Nothing is okay, actually*, and frowned, and she sat down and said she was a good listener, with no idea where she'd gotten the courage.

Sage Abernathy, then like now, had been on the shy side—meek, even. She hated the word, but there had always been something inside her that wouldn't let her speak her mind. She'd always just kept it all in. But with Brent Woodson, she'd been completely herself, the girl she wished she could be with everyone else. Like her parents.

And so, on that bench fifteen years ago, Brent had talked for at least two whole minutes about how his parents were always arguing and he couldn't take another second of it. It was summer, but he still had football practice, so at least that was his escape. And 4-H club, which he was looking forward to the next day. Sage didn't tell him that the only reason she got through 4-H club was because he was in her group. She did tell him all about hating the club with every fiber of her being, that it was bad enough she had to work on her parents' ranch but they made her double down with the club because she kept asking to take painting and drawing classes and they insisted she only needed to immerse herself in the world of agricultural pursuits—not art. Her passion, her dream? They didn't care.

For a half hour, they'd ranted about everything that bothered them. And when they'd gotten up, holding hands, they'd been a couple. After 4-H the next day, they'd kissed for the first time in front of the chicken coop while counting eggs. Sage Abernathy was madly in love. But Brent, though she could tell he liked her, seemed more interested in getting things off his chest than in trying to touch *hers*. Which she absolutely would have let him do had he ever even tried. All they'd done was French kiss. And then one day, Sage finally figured out why Brent always seemed kind of distracted. They had been in the ice cream parlor when Nina Sanchez had come in with her family, and Brent stared so hard at her, his entire being deflating, his expression hangdog, and Sage had suddenly understand that Brent had a thing for Nina, who was dating someone else.

Second fiddle, Sage now remembered thinking. But she'd decided that somehow, someway, she'd use the girl she'd become with only Brent—outspoken, honest, truly herself—to win him over completely. But then the worst thing happened: Her parents found out she had a boyfriend she'd failed to mention. And despite him being the son of the town mayor, they'd insisted she would have to wait till she was eighteen to date. She'd tried to argue, but she was bad at that to start with and they'd been adamant, shutting her down. And then they'd announced they were selling the ranch and moving to Cheyenne since Tenacity seemed to be getting more and more downtrodden and they were sick of waiting for the supposed revitalization of the Tenacity Trail and the dinosaur dig the mayor spoke of but did nothing about.

The most painful part, though? When she told Brent she was moving, he hadn't really seemed to care. *Oh, sorry to hear that, Sage,* he'd said as if he'd been talking about inclement weather canceling their plans. And that had crushed her most of all. She'd never won his heart.

Now here she was, fifteen years later, and just the sight of him stirred up all those old first-love feelings. And the awful awareness that he just hadn't liked her as much as she had him. She wasn't sure how long she'd be in Tenacity—could be a few weeks, could be forever unless she could figure out her next steps and where she might go from here.

What she did know was that she'd certainly not let herself get drawn in by Brent again. First of all, the man was thirty-one and probably married with kids. She wondered if he was a rancher now like he'd wanted to be. Unlike her, he'd planned to defy his parents' expectations of him. They wanted him to become a businessman like his dad, a local politician too. Brent had intended to start his own cattle ranch, his dream. Had he?

Forget it, she told herself. *You saw posters for the swearing-in ceremony when you arrived in town a little while ago, you saw some familiar faces. Including the one you'd hoped to see. So leave.* She turned around to do exactly that, prepared to weave through all the people, back to her car in the lot.

"Sage Abernathy. Wow. You look even more beautiful."

Sage whirled around. Brent.

He was even more handsome just inches away. She could see the beginnings of crow's-feet on the sides of his blue eyes. His face had matured from a teenager into a man. His tall, muscular physique had too. A Stetson covered his blond hair, and he wore a brown leather barn coat over jeans and cowboy boots, a plaid scarf around his neck. She was so dumbstruck for a moment that all she could say was, "Happy New Year."

"And to you," he said with a warm smile. "It's very nice to see you again, Sage. Are you visiting?"

"Not entirely sure. I actually just arrived in Tenacity a half hour ago. I was about to check into the hotel when I noticed the banner at Town Hall announcing the inauguration and thought I'd come by. I was hoping to see some old familiar faces." *Including yours*, she almost added.

"You don't know if you're visiting?" he asked, looking a bit confused.

She inwardly winced. Same old Sage. Letting her parents run roughshod on her to the point that she didn't know what she was doing long term. "My parents are buying a cattle ranch in town. They never expected to return to Tenacity but they read about the plans for a dinosaur park and how that would revitalize the town, and they were reminded of how much they liked it here. They expect me to move here with them, continue on as ranch bookkeeper, help out as needed with chores."

Right now, land could still be snapped up cheap in Tenacity, and her parents loved the idea of buying a ranch five times the size of their current one in Cheyenne before land values quadrupled because of the possible dinosaur park. They assumed she'd follow them and handle the ranch's finances as she'd done since graduating with her business degree—also their idea. But Sage had been getting restless lately. Itchy.

"Ah," he said with a nod. He seemed to understand immediately that she hadn't become the painter she'd once dreamed of being. That she'd done what her parents had wanted for her.

She didn't want to talk about that, though. "They expressed interest in investing in the dinosaur park." Her parents, part of the well-known ranching Abernathy family, were very well off financially, and she'd been touched to hear that they cared about Tenacity, a town that had always been special to her. It was one of the reasons she hadn't put her foot down about staying in Cheyenne and finally going her own way. She'd wanted to help out with the dinosaur park too.

Brent's eyes lit up. "That's great. Barrett and I would love to speak to them about that. It's important that all investors understand that an economic upturn will take at least a year. But we do think the park will be very appealing to visitors across Montana and all nearby states. There's amazing potential for growth."

She nodded. "It was great listening to you and Barrett." She rubbed her mittened hands together. "Chilly out here. Are you planning to head into Town Hall for cake and coffee?" Mayor Garrett had invited the entire town to celebrate the inauguration and all it meant for Tenacity.

Why had she asked that? She should be making excuses to leave. Not practically inviting him to catch up.

"I, uh, I—" He seemed hesitant.

Sage's heart plummeted when it had no business being affected by Brent. This again? Come on. Her gaze dropped to his left hand. Ringless. *Stop caring*, she ordered herself. *Even if he's single, he wasn't really available to you when he* was *your boyfriend. Don't let him be now.*

"Brent, ready to head out for our meeting?" called a male voice.

Sage craned her neck past the throngs of people to see Barrett Deroy standing by the side of the stage. She well remembered Barrett too—and the rumors. Many rumors. That was right before she'd left town.

"One sec," Brent called back, then turned to face her. "Sage, I—you have no idea how much I wish I could, but Barrett and I have had a meeting planned for a while." He seemed about to say something, then clamped his mouth shut. "I'd love to catch up, though. Tomorrow night? Dinner?"

He was asking as though it pained him. Why? She supposed she'd find out what had happened in Brent Woodson's life between the end of summer fifteen years ago and now...if she accepted his invitation.

A middle-aged couple walking by caught her attention because of the way they were staring at Brent.

"We hope you mean what you say," the man blatantly interrupted, eyes narrowed on Brent. "We don't know *what* to think about you."

The woman's chin was raised.

"I absolutely do mean what I say," Brent said to him.

The couple both raised an eyebrow as if to say *We'll see*, then moved along.

"What was that about?" Sage asked. Now that she thought about it, there had been some whispering in the crowd near her while Brent had been talking, but she'd been so focused on him that she hadn't paid attention to the murmurs. What was going on?

Surprise crossed his features. "A long and short story," he said, looking away for a moment. He turned back to her, his gaze soft on hers. "You're staying at the Tenacity Inn? I'll pick you up."

She nodded. "We could go to Castillo's." The casual Mexican restaurant wasn't particularly romantic, which was perfect because this was not a date.

"It's a date," he said with a warm smile, then seemed to freeze as though he certainly hadn't meant to use *that* word.

Interesting, she thought. Something was going on

with Brent Woodson. He was definitely not the same sure-of-himself guy he'd been fifteen years ago. There was a hesitance about him now. She would have expected the opposite, that he'd become even more himself.

She watched him walk toward the stage to meet Barrett. Looking forward to tomorrow night a bit too much, she told herself to be very careful with this…reunion.

Chapter Two

"You really don't have to do this, Vick," Brent told his sister, who was spreading out fresh straw in the pen beside the one he was mucking out. "It's a holiday and you're supposed to be off." Doing basic chores at his ranch always calmed him down, and now, a few hours since the inauguration, he was on an even keel. But his sister should be relaxing, not getting a serious arm workout and holding her nose every ten minutes. When he'd called her to check in earlier and mentioned he'd given his two hands the day off, she insisted on coming over to help.

Victoria Woodson turned and flashed him a weak smile. "You know I'm always happy to help out here. I love this ranch. I can breathe here. Think here. Forget my troubles here."

His heart clenched. Every time he thought of how Victoria had been caught in the slog of his parents' wrongdoings, he wanted to throw something. Hard. At least she, like himself, hadn't known that both their parents had had serious secrets. Not that it was any better to suddenly discover at twenty-seven and thirty-one that everything you thought you knew about your parents was a lie.

"You okay these days?" he asked. He didn't see his sister as often as he'd like. He was always inviting Victoria over to the ranch to see the animals—the sheep were her favorite, and he had a small flock of chickens she liked to rename every time she came by. Or he'd ask her out to lunch or shopping at the general store for a gift for one of his few ranch hands for Christmas or a birthday. But between running the ranch, working with Barrett on the foundation, helping out with coaching the high school football team, and keeping his head down, he didn't have much free time, and Victoria didn't either. She worked at the consignment shop near her apartment above the Tenacity Grocery. He was glad she'd moved out of their parents' house back when the truth had come out. She didn't need to be in the middle of all that tension.

Victoria shoved a swath of her long, dark brown hair behind her ear and used the clean rake to spread out the straw more evenly at the side of the pen. He studied her for a moment. Until you looked closely at the Woodson siblings, you'd never think they were related, given the differences in their coloring. But they had the same big eyes that sloped slightly downward, the same straight nose, the same wavy hair texture. Of course, once he'd found out his mother had had an affair, he'd wondered if one of them wasn't even their dad's kid, but he knew, deep down, they were Woodsons.

"Yeah, I'm okay," she said, leaning her chin on the handle of the rake for a moment. "Just thinking about stuff. I think your talk today at the inauguration will go a long way in changing public perception. You're doing so much for Tenacity, Brent. I know you're my big brother, but I have to say I'm really proud of you." She grabbed another armful of straw and started spreading it out.

"Aw thanks, Vick. That means a lot." The mention of the inauguration reminded him of Sage Abernathy—not that she'd been far from his mind since. "So, I ran into someone today. A blast from the past."

She raised an eyebrow. "Yeah? Who?"

"Sage Abernathy." Her name conjured up her pretty face, her driftwood-brown eyes and long, blond hair, her full pink-red lips.

Victoria's eyes widened. "Sage? Your old girlfriend? She's back?"

He nodded and explained what Sage had told him about her parents buying a ranch here and possibly investing in the dinosaur park. When he'd told Barrett that at their meeting earlier, his partner's eyes had lit up. The Abernathy family was well-known in Tenacity. If they were publicly investing and talking up the park, other donations could follow. Brent was hopeful too.

Victoria put the rake away in the storage cabinet by the door, then wrapped her scarf more tightly around her neck. "Too bad you guys broke up. I remember she was so nice."

"I wasn't exactly great boyfriend material back then."

She frowned. "Well, you were always a great brother."

Brent felt something tight loosen in his shoulders, in his stomach. "That's a really nice thing to say, Vick. Especially when 'great' isn't something I hear about myself much."

"I hate how things are now," Victoria said, then sucked in a breath and looked up at the sky, a beautiful blue sky for the first of the year, even if things felt gray at the moment. "I hate that our family reputation is destroyed. I hate that Mom and Dad are divorcing. What was the point of living a lie for the past fifteen years, keeping those huge secrets, if they're not even going to try anymore?"

That surprised him, and he stared at his sister. "You think they *could* work things out?"

She shrugged. "I don't know. I mean, they stayed together for fifteen years knowing each other's worst secrets. And it's not like things have improved the past six months. Still, they've both stayed in town—facing the music together. There's that, at least."

"Yeah, true. I'd like to think that's about us, Vick. We're here. Despite the really bad stuff they've both done, maybe when it comes right down to it, *we* matter to them. Maybe that means there's hope for them as human beings."

Tears welled in her eyes, and she slowly nodded. "I just wish..." She stopped talking and leaned against the side of the barn door.

He got it. He *just wished* too.

He was sure one of his parents would file the papers. Right after the truth came out, Clifford and June had both stayed in the big house in town, but Vicky had told him that his mom moved into the guest room and they were barely speaking. Things were bad enough before Clifford Woodson had gotten involved in making sure his buddy Marty had become mayor of Tenacity last fall. But once he made things even worse for the family by clearly getting involved in those dirty dealings, June Woodson had washed her hands and insisted her husband move out. Clifford had dug in his heels, and they still lived together in a kind of cold war. According to his mother, they were never in the same room at the same time and communicated solely through terse texts.

Brent let out a sigh. There was *a lot* to get through.

Vicky pushed off the wall and peered into the next stall, grabbing the mucking rake. "Do you think you and Dad will mend fences?"

"I don't know. I'm so angry at him, you know?"

She nodded. "Yeah, same."

And their father was unrepentant. The sobbing always seemed like either crocodile tears or because he just felt really sorry for himself. *Poor me, poor Clifford.*

"And what about Mom?" Brent asked gently.

Victoria shrugged. "That's really hard to think about. I mean, she was planning on running off with Barrett's dad. Did she not care about us?"

"I still have so many questions for her," Brent said. "But honestly, do I want to know the answers? I'm not sure."

"I hear you on that," Victoria said, frowning.

"What I really want to know, and what she's never

been able to answer, is why she didn't return the money to the town. Why did she leave it hidden under that boulder at the old house on Juniper Road for fifteen years? It makes no sense."

Victoria turned away, and he realized this was all too much for her.

"Hey," he said softly. "Let's stop talking about the past. Things are looking up."

She turned toward him and nodded, but her face and shoulders were tense, like she might start crying any minute.

"Do you think they'll get in trouble? Like criminal trouble? It's been six months and nothing's come up about charges or anything like that. They won't be prosecuted?"

Brent lifted up his Stetson and ran a hand through his hair. "The statute of limitations is past, so I don't think either will face prosecution. Even with Dad messing around with the election. There's just not any substantial proof he did. Just people's gut—and mine."

Victoria frowned and nodded, stuffing her hands in the pocket of her down jacket. "I'd better get going. I'm meeting Cassie Trent for dinner later. She very nicely still makes time for her old friend even though she's engaged now."

Brent smiled. "Go have fun. Eat something good. Call me if you ever need to talk. Or just want to walk in silence with your big bro beside you."

She suddenly wrapped her arms around him in an unexpected bear hug. "I love you, Brent. And you *are* the best. I don't care what anyone in this town thinks."

Huh. "I'm working on not caring," he said.

She gave him a half smile and jogged over to her little car.

At least he had Victoria. And she had him. Their parents might be all over the place, but he and Vick were the good Woodsons, and they'd rebuild the family name.

That determination, coupled with how much he was looking forward to seeing Sage Abernathy tomorrow for dinner, was all he needed right now.

After leaving the inauguration, Sage had skipped the coffee-and-cake reception. Seeing Brent again, her reaction to him, the fact that they were getting together tomorrow night, had knocked her off-kilter, and she'd just wanted to go check into her hotel room. She now sat in the chair by the window overlooking Central Avenue, which was teeming with people who were leaving Tenacity Town Hall.

Since most folks had been at the reception, she hadn't run into anyone she used to know in the lobby of the hotel, except for Ruby McKinley, who worked the front desk and had checked her in. Sage remembered Ruby from high school; the woman was now a mom of two and married to Julian Sanchez—Nina Sanchez's brother. Ruby showed her photos of her kiddos—a little girl who looked just like her and a baby boy she and her husband had adopted last year. Ruby asked if she had kids with the warm smile of someone who'd love to see photos, and Sage had felt that familiar pang at having to say *No, not yet, but hopefully one day...*

Sage's thirtieth birthday had been a little rough because she wasn't even on the road to where she thought
she'd be by now. Married to a great guy. Pregnant with
her *second* child. A stay-at-home mom and painting
still lifes and landscapes in her home art studio during her children's naps—paintings she'd sold at craft
fairs or even her own show at an art gallery.

Sigh. At thirty she was still living out her parents'
expectations for her. Why? That was what she'd never
understood. As a kid, as a teenager, fine. But once
she'd hit mid-twenties, she couldn't put where she was
in life on anyone but herself. She just didn't get why
she didn't make changes. Afraid to rock the boat? In
her family, in her own everyday world?

Sage stared out the window, Brent's handsome face
floating into her mind. She was still so attracted to
him. Fifteen years ago, she'd thought he was the cutest boy in school. Now a man at thirty-one, he pulled
her toward him like a magnet even more. She got up
and looked up and down the street, seeing many places
she and Brent had gone together in their short-lived
summer romance. She'd never forget sitting on the
benches in the park, under the big trees, Brent telling
her one day she'd be living her dream, he was sure of
it. She'd felt so happy and full because she'd believed
him, which had made her realize she believed in herself. What had happened to that girl?

She had to get out of here or she'd go stir-crazy. A
walk would do her good, even though it was cold. She
changed into on a thick wool Fair Isle sweater to keep
warm. She'd brought a week's worth of basics, includ-

ing a wrap dress and a pair of nice pants, nice boots and her cowboy boots, since she wasn't sure how long she'd be staying. Her parents would be arriving in a few days, and she'd check out the property they planned to buy, spend a little time with them, and then head back to Cheyenne. She'd have to go home regardless of whether she moved with her parents or not, since all her stuff was at the ranch there.

She bundled up and locked her door, then headed downstairs to the lobby, which was a little busier than earlier.

"Sage Abernathy!"

She turned at the female voice and immediately recognized Daniella McMann, an old high school acquaintance with curly, red hair and green eyes. She held a baby in her arms—eight, nine months, maybe—with drooping eyes fighting sleep.

Sage couldn't stop staring at the precious little girl. She was struck with a familiar yearning—baby fever. It happened a lot lately. She stifled a sigh. Thirty, childless, and not even *dating*.

There's only one way to get the things you want. Go after them.

She had to change. Period. She had be her own woman.

"Daniella, you look just the same," Sage said. "It's so nice to see you. And who is this beautiful little girl?"

They quickly caught up. Daniella was married to "the man of her dreams," her eight-month-old daughter, Layla, was a great napper, and she had the mother-in-law from hell. She ranted about the woman, who criticized everything from Daniella's cooking to the brand of diapers she bought.

"Ugh, sorry," Sage said. "Maybe I should be glad I'm not married yet," she added with a commiserating smile, more to make herself feel better than anything.

"Oh trust me, I'd rather have the mother-in-law from hell than be *single*," Daniella said, mock-shivering. "Besides, then I'd be all alone and I wouldn't have my darling baby girl." She gave the baby a snuggle. "You must be so lonely!"

Of all the people she could have run into…

Before Sage could even counter that—not that it wasn't true—Daniella went on. "So, were you at the inauguration? Did you see your old boyfriend up on-stage? Honestly, I don't know if I give Barrett Deroy credit or not for even *talking* to Brent Woodson, let alone partnering with him. I mean, Barrett must be a naive idiot—there's no way Brent didn't know. Come *on*." She added an eye roll, shifting her baby in her arms. The baby's eyes opened, her face flushing, and she let out a wail, then another. Daniella rocked her a bit, but the baby kept screaming. "Time to get this one down for her nap. Nice to run into you!" And with that, she was thankfully gone.

Okay, what was this all about? Given the encounter with the couple in the park, the whispering, and now this, something had happened. But what?

Sage felt her eyes widen. Could this be about what happened fifteen years ago? When the Deroys left town? A chill ran up her spine. When she'd moved to Cheyenne, Sage had tried to keep up with a few girl-friends, but the relationships had all faded to nothing after a few months. She had no idea what had become of that old story—the Deroys leaving town because Barrett had supposedly stolen thousands from the town. He was back, clearly. And no one seemed to be giving him side-eye or whispering about *him*.

Fifteen years ago, when that gossip had spread, Sage had had a few suspicions of her own that had nothing to do with Barrett Deroy. She'd thought about talking to Brent about it all, but one, she hadn't been sure of anything, and two, every time she even thought about raising the subject, she'd imagine Brent's face—angry, hurt, refusing to speak to her again. So she'd kept putting off saying anything and then her family had moved, making it all moot. She didn't have proof—just a bad feeling.

Suddenly, the last thing Sage wanted to do was walk around Tenacity and see how the town had changed in the past fifteen years. It seemed clear from the little she had seen, and what she'd heard at the inauguration, that change was only starting to happen now. When had Barrett come back to Tenacity? Recently, she assumed—the past few months. And why were people down on Brent? He hadn't done anything wrong, had he?

She decided to pick up lunch to-go from the Silver Spur Café, take it back to her room, and do a Google search for Woodson, Tenacity, and Deroy. Maybe she'd learn something.

She had so many questions, but she wasn't sure she wanted the answers.

Because it was possible that the secrets Sage had kept for fifteen years had caused trouble she hadn't even considered.

Chapter Three

The next night, when Brent pulled open the door to the Tenacity Inn and saw Sage sitting in a chair by one of the windows in the lobby, his breath caught. It was more than how beautiful she looked—her long, wavy blond hair loose past her shoulders, her pink-red lips with a slight shimmer. She felt so familiar, despite the years that had separated them. She smiled and stood when she saw him.

"I like your coat," he said. He realized just how nervous he was if *that* was his greeting. Like a tongue-tied teenager. But he did like it—brown suede with fringe. She wore a long silver necklace with a turquoise pendant, a camel-colored sweater, dark jeans, and cowboy boots. Sage reminded him of a country-western singer.

Her smile deepened. "Thanks. I like your hat."

He tipped it at her. "And thank *you*. I'm rarely not wearing one."

"I remember," she said. "Except when you had to trade it for a helmet."

"Well, now I stick to coaching football, though sometimes a bunch of us will get together to play a pickup game in the park."

They gazed at each other for a moment, something tender and curious in her brown eyes.

"I'm starving," she said. "I'm so glad we're having dinner. I'm looking forward to catching up."

"Me too." He wished Tenacity had more restaurants for dinner, but Castillo's for Mexican or T. Bones for steaks were pretty much it. Seeing Sage again after all these years warranted something special, and the steakhouse seemed a little too casual with its sawdust-decorated floors whereas Castillo's was definitely festive. "I have a craving for enchiladas. Or steak fajitas and their great rice."

"I can *always* go for Mexican," she said as she buttoned her coat and tightened her wool scarf.

As they were heading toward the door, a group of people was coming in, a double date of couples a little older than him. And they were all staring at Brent. Dammit.

Come on, not in front of Sage. Throw me a bone. By now, he was sure she'd heard the whole sorry story about his family, but he still didn't want to have to talk about all that first thing. He'd much rather hear about her life in Cheyenne. If she was seeing anyone…

"Brent Woodson," a guy who looked familiar said. He might have been a few grades up from Brent in school. John or Jake, something like that.

Brent stopped and lifted his chin. He had to stop doing that—taking a defensive stance. *If the guy gets offensive, you'll handle it Brent 2.0–style.* Which meant without tough-guy bluster. Without relying on his size and name to do half the work for him. He was still tall and muscular, of course, but he didn't throw around his football player's build the way he used to, even when confronted. And these days, all his last name would get him was a sneer, if not a punch in the face.

The guy extended his hand. "I think you and Deroy are going to turn this town around, and I'm all for it. You guys and Mayor Garrett. I'm here for it." He smiled, and the group behind him, two women and another guy, all murmured in agreement.

Warmth hit Brent in the chest. He wasn't too used to that. "Thanks. You have no idea how much I appreciate that."

The guy nodded, and his group headed toward the elevator.

Huh. That put him in an even better headspace as he and Sage headed out into the chilly January evening. The sun had set over an hour ago, but the occasional streetlamp and the Christmas lights that still brightened up downtown illuminated their path. Plus the moon shone brightly in the sky, a crescent, which Brent had always thought meant good luck.

So far, so good tonight.

"That was nice," Sage said as they walked toward Castillo's. "I'm sure you get a lot of that."

He'd been relieved, surprised, and grateful after their talk at the inauguration yesterday at how many nods and fist-bumps he'd gotten. He wasn't sure whether it was the sight of him and Barrett together that had helped change public opinion of him or whether they'd liked what he had to say yesterday, but the interaction just now was making it clear both had a great effect.

Still, he wasn't up for talking about the past with Sage just yet.

"How did you spend your day?" he asked as they crossed the street. "Visiting with old friends?"

"To be honest, I don't really have any left here. Fifteen years is a long time to be away. I thought some friendships would stick, but they didn't."

I know how that is, he thought, glad it hadn't burst out of his mouth.

"My closest girlfriend from Tenacity—you might remember her, Mandy—she moved away the year after I did to Washington State. We still talk at least once a week."

"I always had a tight group of friends. But when—" He stopped talking, stopped walking, and looked at Sage. So much for not talking about the past. Maybe a part of him wanted to get it over with. "I didn't realize that I was a jerk until pretty recently. Like six months ago. I also didn't realize that some of my buddies were even bigger jerks than I ever was. Let's just say I've learned a lot about myself, about people in general."

She reached for his hand. "I know what happened, Brent. The whispers and comments set me on a Google search. I read all the local stories. My goodness, Brent. I'm so sorry."

He could have hugged her. "It means a lot to hear that. I don't think a single person has actually said those words to me. Because most folks still think I'm guilty by association. That I knew and kept my mouth shut, or worse—that I rejoiced in it all. 'Yeah, Dad, frame Barrett and blackmail his family to leave town so then I can go after his girlfriend.'"

He saw Sage flinch, and wished he hadn't said it. Some of the old Brent was still too close to the surface sometimes. He'd always have to work on that. Think about others first. Their feelings.

"Having Barrett on your side must have helped, though, right?" she asked.

"No one was more surprised than I was when he extended a hand and asked me to partner with him on the foundation to revitalize Tenacity. Some people just can't get past thinking I must have known, though. And the whole thing is just…ugly. An affair. Theft. A frame job. Blackmail. One family run out of town, their reputation destroyed. Another family with sickening secrets, and their kids—a twelve-year-old and a sixteen-year-old—completely clueless." He shook his head.

Sage bit her lip. He wondered what she was thinking. How he could have been so blind to his parents' real selves, what they were capable of.

Sage had seen *her* parents for what they were— very strict, demanding, uncompromising. Why hadn't *he* seen the depths of his mother's unhappiness in her marriage to his father? Why hadn't he realized how low his father would stoop to get his way? Had his parents been that good at hiding things? Or had Brent just been too self-absorbed to care about anything other than his own golden-boy world?

He was so grateful Victoria had been so young then. She was a sensitive, caring person who always seemed to notice when someone was upset or needed a shoulder, but at twelve years old, all that had thankfully gone over her head.

His chest felt tight. It was time to change the subject.

"I talked so much I never gave you the chance to answer my question," he said, resuming walking. "What have you been doing since you arrived? Half of yesterday and today?"

"I did a lot of driving around town. Past my school, my family's old house. I sat parked on the street in front a long time. Just thinking. Trying to figure out some stuff."

"Like what?" he asked. He stopped for a second. "I understand if that's too personal. Until yesterday, I hadn't seen you in fifteen years, but in a lot of ways, it feels like we've always been in touch."

That wasn't quite true. Sure, he felt a connection to Sage—a surprising connection, given that he hadn't realized what he had all those years ago. He was well aware she wasn't the same girl she'd been then. Just as he wasn't the same guy. In fact, he'd say very little remained of that Brent Woodson.

"Can I ask you something else too? Something…a little strange?"

"Of course," she said, tilting her head. Waiting.

"I know why girls liked me so much back in high school. Mr. Popularity. Football player. Son of the mayor. Nice house in town. But girls I dated before you *only* cared about that stuff. No one got to know me. So I guess I'm just wondering, given that you didn't seem to care about any of that—what *did* you see in me?"

"Not gonna lie, Brent. I thought you were the cutest boy in school. And yes, I was dazzled by all the trappings you just mentioned. But from that first time we talked on that park bench, I knew who you *were*. Honest. Kind. Interesting. Sensitive. Trustworthy. I felt like I could tell you anything."

Warmth spread through his chest. He was so touched, so moved, that he couldn't speak for a second. Brent Woodson—*honest? Sensitive?* He sucked in a breath. If it were appropriate to kiss her right now, he would.

"You were always so easy to talk to, Brent. I'm not surprised we're falling right back into that. Asking each other real questions."

He nodded. "Exactly how I feel."

She gave him something of a smile as they kept walking. "So to answer your question—what I'm trying to figure out is, what I'm doing, where I'm going. Am I moving to Tenacity with my parents? Handling the books at the new ranch? Just doing what I've always done?"

Ah. She seemed to be at a crossroads. Same old path or something more. "If you could do anything, what would it be?"

She glanced at him, and he could see her face brightening. "I'd have my own painting studio in my home. I'd live on a beautiful small ranch—but just for the land. No animals. Well, except for a horse. And two dogs. A few cats. And whatever wild critters are around. I'd live close to my parents, even though they're not the easiest people to be around. In fact, I think if I were really living the way I wanted, I'd want to spend more time with them instead of less."

"Do you resent them?" he asked. How easy was this? The talking. They *had* been close back then, closer than he really understood. So much so that he knew exactly what she meant now, what the history was and that it clearly hadn't changed. He realized that even if he'd been distracted by his unrequited feelings for someone else, he and Sage had been true friends.

She seemed to be thinking about his question. "I resent *myself*, and sometimes I blame them for that when *I'm* the problem. If that makes a lick of sense."

"There *are* fifteen years to cover, so I'll definitely need some details," he said with a gentle smile. They'd arrived at the restaurant. "Hold that thought," he said, pulling open the door. She walked in and he followed, Yolanda Castillo greeting them with a warm smile and with two menus.

The restaurant was dimly lit, wooden booths lining both walls, a bar in the back. Mexican decor brightened up the walls, painted a warm orange. Castillo's had been around for as long as Brent could remember. His parents had always been food snobs but even they loved Castillo's delicious, authentic Mexican food and often got takeout. He could remember being as young as five and having their bean-and-cheese burritos.

As Yolanda led them to an empty booth at the far end, the other diners definitely looked up and noticed them, and he heard a few whispers. Nothing bad, at least. He was pretty sure one woman they passed said,

I think they used to date. He definitely heard someone say: *I still don't know what to think about Brent.*

He was glad their booth was the last at the end, where they'd have some privacy.

"That must be tough to deal with," she said, upping her chin out at the restaurant. "You okay?"

He nodded. "It's a lot better than it was even a couple of months ago. And yesterday helped a lot."

Yolanda's youngest son, Enrique, came over for their drink orders, and they each chose margaritas—frozen for Sage, on the rocks for him. They were still perusing the menu when she returned with the tart drinks, a basket of chips, and salsa. She lit the candle and said she'd be back in a few minutes to take their orders.

"Remember when we came here?" he asked.

She grinned and looked up from the menu. "For our monthiversary."

They didn't have a lot of free time back then, even during the summer, because he still had football practice and Sage was expected to work full-time at her family's ranch, but he could remember thinking if they actually lasted a month, he'd take her out to dinner. They'd lasted almost three. And he hadn't appreciated a moment of it. Like he said: jerk.

Once they'd ordered—barbacoa enchiladas for him and a chicken burrito for her—he held up his drink and so did she.

"To reunions," he said. There was more he could add, but right now, that they were together was all that mattered.

She smiled and they clinked glasses, both of them taking a sip.

"What did you mean before—that *you're* the problem?" he asked, swiping a chip through the salsa.

She frowned and seemed lost in thought for a few seconds. "As you know, when I was a teen, I was pretty meek. I did what my parents told me to do. When I asked my mom if I could take painting lessons at the community center, she said I should spend my time on practical pursuits that would lead to a bright future for me at the family ranch. And I just never felt I could challenge that. They insisted I major in agricultural business in college, so I did. I got to take art classes for electives, and that's what got me through all those boring classes on animal husbandry and ranch finance." She smiled. "No offense."

He reached his hand across the table to squeeze hers for a moment. "None taken in the slightest. I always admired that you were interested in art, that you were so talented. I loved your drawings."

Her smile lit up her face. "Those were just pencil doodles."

"*Great* pencil doodles. Remember the drawing you did of me?" he asked. "When we went to the Silver Spur Café after school and both had turkey BLTs?" He hadn't thought of that drawing in a long time. To the point that he wasn't even sure he still had it. He'd look for it.

"I remember drawing your face and thinking you were so gorgeous," she said, a slight flush coming to her cheeks.

He smiled. "If I were drawing you right now, you'd come out looking like Mrs. Potato Head, but I'd be thinking you were the prettiest woman in Montana."

She laughed, her brown eyes twinkling, and she smiled in a way that told him she liked that compliment, that it had been welcome. He felt something inside him stir. Something good and sweet and full of possibilities.

"Well, now that I'm thirty and have been a grown woman for quite some time, I seem kind of stuck. I've been living at the family ranch and handling the finances for the past eight years. And in my free time, I seem to help out on the ranch with chores instead of taking art classes. Maybe I use it as an excuse—I don't know. I do some painting, and I've even sold a few of my landscapes on my online shop through a popular website. But..." She paused, her pretty face showing how conflicted she was. "So that's what I mean. That I'm doing the same old thing I've always done is on *me*. Not my parents."

"Maybe you just never felt entitled to your dream," he said. "And you've been living a certain life for eight years and it's what you're used to and know. I get it."

She gave him an appreciative smile and took a sip of her margarita, and he could see he'd gotten that right.

Enrique came over with their entrées, which smelled and looked delicious. They dug in, agreeing that the food was as great as ever. They even tried a bite of each other's meals. If this dinner went on forever, that would be fine with him.

"But now that my parents are selling the Cheyenne

ranch and moving here…" She took a bite of her burrito and then set it down. "It's shaken me up in a good way. Forced me to really question what *I* want for a change. I know I want to focus more on my watercolors. Who knows—maybe if I devote myself to it full-time, I can earn enough to get by. Or work part-time to supplement. I don't need much. I never have."

He realized he was staring at her, and cut into his enchiladas. "I think you should follow your heart, Sage. Give painting its real due."

She smiled so warmly that he felt it in his toes. "So tell me about yourself. Did you go to school for agricultural management like you'd always wanted?"

He nodded. "My parents wanted me to study business and follow in my dad's footsteps, but since business courses were such a big part of the agricultural program, they didn't give me a hard time even though they were paying the tuition. And now I have my own cattle ranch."

"I really admire that you followed your heart and became the rancher you always dreamed of. Your parents had expectations of you, but you went your own way, walked your own path."

"Well, that might be because I always put myself first, Sage. I was pretty selfish. I understand things a little better these days."

"Did your folks help you get started?" she asked.

He shook his head. "No way. My dad said Tenacity was a hard town to make it in, and we'd made it, so why would I go into such a rough business that could fold like so many other ranches in town? I told him I'd start slow and build my way up, and he told me I was nuts and wished me luck—sarcastically. Once I started college, I got a part-time job working at a ranch and learned everything from the ground up. After I graduated, I worked at another huge prosperous ranch for a couple of years, and then I was able to buy a failing ranch on good land. I worked my butt off and turned the place around. Big Sky Ranch does pretty well."

"Big Sky Ranch," she repeated. "I love that. Big sky, big dreams."

He could barely take his eyes off her pretty face. But his smiled faded a bit when he realized there were just crumbs left on their plates. That dinner was over. They'd caught up. So now what?

Prolong. He didn't want to put her on the spot, though. If he invited her for a nightcap, that would sound like a date. He liked the idea of that, but why start something when she might not even be sticking around Tenacity? And if she did decide to move with her parents, getting reinvolved with him wouldn't exactly be a great way for people to get to know her again. He was a liability. He should leave well enough alone.

"I'll get the check, and then I'll walk you back to the inn," he said with an inward sigh. Dammit.

She certainly didn't look disappointed that he hadn't suggested a drink somewhere. "Okay."

Of course she wasn't. This was just a catch-up dinner, not a date. They'd had a nice meal, they'd talked, and that was that.

They got their check, and he insisted on paying, glad when she relented on splitting it, then he helped her on with her coat, the scent of her perfume intoxicating him.

No, he was not ready for this night to end. But something told him it was the right thing to do. His life was a disaster now. He was making strides to change things, but that wasn't happening so fast. Sage didn't need to be pulled into that. And she needed to figure out her path, which was probably not Tenacity.

The thing was, he'd lost her once and now here she was, standing within kissing distance from him. And kissing her was what he really wanted to do.

And exactly what he *shouldn't* do.

As they walked back to the hotel, Sage was going over ways she could suggest a drink—maybe at the Grizzly Bar, which was nearby—without sounding like she was turning their reunion dinner into a date. When Brent had said he'd walk her back, her heart had sunk. She'd thought there was romance in the air, but maybe she'd misread things.

Brent was quiet on the way, but they were walking fast since it was cold. The inn wasn't very far, but now she wished they had a few miles to go. She wasn't ready for their night to end.

As they reached the hotel, she realized that if she wanted to start asserting herself, there was no time like now.

"How about a nightcap?" she asked. "Grizzly Bar?" She kept her tone casual, but even she could hear how hopeful she was. It was probably all over her face. "I've never been there, of course, since I was way underage when I lived here. But I like the name." She smiled awkwardly, no doubt her heart practically beating out of her chest.

"Sounds great," he said, his big smile making it clear he meant it. "I've spent a little *too* much time at the Grizzly over the years. But that's because I like it. A beer sounds great. And to be honest, I wasn't ready to say goodbye. I'm having a great time, Sage."

Her heart gave a little leap. "Me too."

He smiled again, his handsome face lighting up, and they headed to the Grizzly Bar. It was next door to the Silver Spur Café, where she'd been plenty as a teen. Brent pulled open the can't-miss orange door for her, and heads turned to see who was coming in. Sage was now a little more used to the curious looks and whispers. Her heart went out to Brent, and she wanted to shout, *He didn't know. Back off!*

She could tell from some of those sitting at the long bar or waiting their turn to shoot pool that they were curious about her and Brent being together. Their romance had been short lived, but folks in Tenacity had a long memory. The Abernathys were a well-known family, as were the Woodsons, so they'd stood out. Even though Sage was a from different branch of Abernathys than the ones most folks knew of, the name was its own introduction—prominent, wealthy, ranching. Which was exactly how her parents had found out she was dating. She was happy that Brent had been her first boyfriend, her first kiss—even her first heartache, because she'd felt so much for him.

As they headed in, she looked around. The Grizzly

Bar was a classic Western honky-tonk, complete with
a large chandelier made from antlers. They found an
empty booth, and a barmaid came over to take their
orders: beers for both.

"Nice to see you," the middle-aged woman said to
Brent with a no-nonsense nod.

Brent gave a nod and smile back.

"That's the second time today someone has been
positive," Sage pointed out. "The third, if you count
the guy right after the inauguration."

"You're clearly a good-luck charm."

She smiled, then whispered, "I'm so curious, Brent.
When you called to me at the inauguration yesterday, I
was kind of surprised you even recognized me."

"Surprised? Why?"

"Well…" She was glad the barmaid was back with
their drinks to give herself some time to answer. Why
had she said all that? She supposed it had been poking the back of her mind—how they'd left things fifteen years ago.

She held up her glass and he clinked hers with his,
then she sipped her beer. "When we had to break up,
you didn't seem too put out. And when I left town, you
texted a few times and then you just stopped."

"You know that saying 'you don't what you have till
it's gone'? That's it exactly. Looking back, it's easy for
me to see that I had no business dating anyone when I
was still hung up on another girl. I didn't even really
know Nina Sanchez back then—I just thought she was
pretty." He smiled and shook his head. "I was an idiot
back then, Sage. I say that in all seriousness."

Sage smiled. "I wasn't toasting to you saying you were an idiot."

He smiled too. "You'd have the right. But every day, I work on myself. Thinking before I speak. Caring about how others feel. Can you imagine going through pretty much your entire life only thinking of yourself? That was me until six months ago. And both reasons are why people think I was complicit in what my dad did—"

"Because you'd benefit from Barrett being run out of town," she finished for him. She shook her head. "That's awful."

"Well, I get it. At the time, I couldn't wrap my small mind around the fact that Nina would want a farrier's son over the *mayor's* son. I'm *long* over my crush, but I have to say, I admire Nina's unwavering faith in Barrett over the years. That's real love."

Sage nodded, her chest warming. She liked that he'd commented on that, that he knew that. Brent seemed to be harder on himself than anyone, but he also seemed to understand what love was. "Definitely."

"All these years, I believed Barrett had stolen that money," Brent added. "Ruined Tenacity's chances for a better future. And the whole time, it was my *mother* who was the thief. Talk about a double whammy. I had to admit I was wrong about Barrett—*and* somehow accept what my mother did. The affair, planning to run away, leave her kids." He tilted his head back and let out a breath. "When the truth first came out six months ago, I asked my mom why she didn't just return the money after her plans were thwarted. Why she just left the money under that boulder. She could have given it back to the town."

Sage swallowed. This was a very sensitive subject. All the more so because Sage had her own ideas about why. "What did your mom say?" She leaned forward, very curious what June Woodson's response had been.

Brent sipped his beer, then set the bottle down. "She said that the very day she was set to meet Barrett Sr. to leave town together, the money had *disappeared*. My dad had confronted her that day about overhearing her talking on the phone about her affair. So that's how he found out about the plan. My mom always assumed Cliff found the money and buried it. But he always denied it."

That didn't surprise Sage. She believed that someone else had found out about the affair and the plan, and had stolen the money and buried it.

She didn't have proof, though. Just speculation based on...a few things said long ago. Last night, when she'd read about what had happened in the news articles, some old conversations had come back to her. And she'd suddenly understood a few things better than she had fifteen years ago.

But right now, at least, Sage would keep all that to herself. She couldn't very well throw around accusations. At this point, her take on what might have really happened wouldn't help anything. And might actually do some damage.

"Who knows with those two?" Brent suddenly said, glancing out the window. She could tell he was a bit lost in thought. "Honestly, I don't know what to think about why my mom left the money there all these years. Anyway, there's something I do really want to know."

Sage leaned forward. "What?"

Brent took a slug of his beer. "How I could have ignored the now crystal clear signs that my father had no moral compass. Six months ago, he promised to change—and I believed him. And what did he turn around and do? Help fix the mayoral election so that his buddy Marty Moore would win." He let out a frustrated breath. "I confronted him, and of course he sobbed and lied and swore he had nothing to do with that, that JenniLynn's husband didn't want her being mayor to distract her from the family so her husband was the sole culprit in helping Marty win. But I just assume my dad had a hand in it."

Sage's heart clenched for him. "And that's why you give the way people treat you so much grace. Because you understand someone saying they're going to change only for it to be a lie."

The pain on his face broke her heart. "Exactly." His shoulders sank in defeat. How she wished she could go over and hug him. But she didn't feel that was her place.

Especially because she was hiding something from him. Something she'd long believed about his family.

His wounds were still raw, and she understood why. Even as a teenager, she had been aware of the dysfunction in Brent's family based on what he'd told her. But though Brent talked a lot about his parents' arguing and how they sometimes slept in separate rooms and had cold wars and that they'd tried to convince him to go into business and not ranching, that he should live up to

the lofty Woodson name, he'd still believed they were
solid gold, great people. He'd been proud of his family.

That he was so torn apart by the truth was no surprise to Sage.

As she took a gulp of her juice, she wondered what
would have happened if she'd talked to him about
his mother's affair. There had been gossip but Brent
never mentioned it, and she'd figured he actually hadn't
heard the rumors. He was a big man on campus, and
she could see how people were careful not to whis-
per around him. But she'd heard the talk—about June
Woodson and a man named Cheeto, who drove the ice
cream truck around town.

Except Sage had known then that Cheeto wasn't
June Woodson's lover. She knew because she'd actually
seen June and Barrett Sr. in a passionate embrace in an
alley doorway one night when she'd been coming back
from her friend's house. She'd had to squint through
the dark, foggy night that they probably thought had
given them cover, but she'd seen them. She'd *known*.
And she'd kept it to herself for several reasons.

But the truth about that had been out for a while
now. It was her *other* suspicion, that there was much
more to who'd found the stolen money and had buried
it under that boulder than Brent knew.

Should she even tell him what she thought? How
could it possibly help anything? It would only hurt
him. And who knew what can of worms it would open?

A chill ran up Sage's spine. How could she hope
to rekindle something with Brent Woodson when she
was hiding an explosive secret from him? Secrets had

destroyed the life he'd once known. And now her *own* might destroy the new one he was building.

She bit her lip and looked out the window with no idea what to do.

All she knew was that she'd better call it a night.

Chapter Four

The next morning, Brent stood at his kitchen counter, pouring coffee for his guests. Barrett Deroy and Seth Taylor sat at his kitchen table, talking dinosaur bones. These days, it was one of Brent's favorite topics of conversation.

He was pumped for this meeting. Seth, one of the millionaire heirs to the Taylor Beef empire out in Bronco, had come to Tenacity a couple of months ago to visit his brother, Daniel. Seth had gotten very interested in the dinosaur bones found in town and was among the first to agree to invest in the dig and a theme park. It helped that he'd fallen for a local paleontologist who lived and breathed all things dinosaur, and now he and Andrea Spence were living together, and Tenacity was his home. The two men at the table were both madly in love with their women, and Brent could see how it had changed them, softened their edges, expanded their way of thinking and looking at things. Brent could use a little of that in his own life.

When he'd gotten home from the too-short nightcap at the Grizzly Bar—Sage had called it a night after one drink—he'd just wanted to think about her, all they'd talked about, all he'd felt. He had to force himself into his home office to do some research for the meeting. He'd been so distracted, though. By the image of her beautiful face floating into his mind. By how easy it was to talk to her about what was going on in his life. He was able to open up to her without being judged. She was also one of the rare people who'd liked Brent then and seemed to like him now, despite how different he was. She'd seen the good parts of him, parts he wasn't even aware of back then. That was the guy she'd fallen for. And that meant a lot to him.

For a minute there, when she'd invited him for the drink, he'd thought she might be interested romantically, but after barely a half hour, she'd said she should be getting back to the inn. Some cold water had been tossed on his hopes for rekindling their relationship, but that was probably for the best. If she ended up staying in Tenacity, getting involved with him would color how people looked at her, and she didn't need that. And if she went back to Cheyenne or somewhere else to pursue her life as an artist, he wouldn't want to hold her back. Especially when his life still seemed in flux.

He brought the mugs of coffee, creamer, and sugar over on a tray and set it down in the center of the table next to the platter of treats he'd picked up from the bakery. "My sister gave me these chocolate-hazelnut swizzle sticks," he said, pointing to the little canister of them. "I have no idea if you're supposed to just stir the coffee with them or eat them too."

"Well, I'm the professional risk-taker here," Seth said, "So I'll take a chomp, and we'll see if I get sick or not." Brent admired the way Seth, in his early forties, barged head-on into the unknown—a new town, a new love, new investment opportunities. Even a potential stomachache.

Barrett laughed. "*Chomp* is a good word from an investor in a dinosaur park." He exposed his teeth and let out a roar.

Brent cracked up. "*Dig* in to the bakery stuff," he said, pointing to the treats on the table, everything from scones to muffins to Danishes. "Okay, I think we exhausted the dinosaur puns." How good it felt to be so comfortable with people again, to feel welcomed and part of things, especially something as vital as the town's revitalization efforts. Brent used to take just about everything for granted. Not anymore.

They fixed their coffees and grabbed their baked goods. Seth took a bite of the swizzle stick and declared it delicious; then they settled in to talk about where the foundation was. Money-wise, they were getting there, but attracting a few more investors was key.

"So, Brent," Seth said, picking up his mug, "Barrett mentioned that you'd told him the Abernathys might want to invest?"

Brent sipped his coffee and then nodded. "I ran into Sage Abernathy at the inauguration, and she told me her parents expressed interest. They're due in town in the next couple of days to buy a working ranch."

Seth's eyes lit up. "Great to hear. I know the Abernathy family well. My sister Charlotte is married to Sage's cousin, Billy Abernathy—they live out in Bronco. If I'm not mistaken, Sage and Billy share a great-grandpa, but that's a big family, so I might have that wrong. Anyway, if Sage's parents are in, the project is all but guaranteed to move forward. I'd be happy to reach out to them since we have that family connection. I'm not sure if Charlotte or Billy will have her parents' number, so if you can get that from Sage, that would be great."

"Will do," Brent said to Seth. He knew better than to suggest himself for the job of talking investing with the Abernathys. Sage's parents hadn't been his biggest fans fifteen years ago. Even if they'd thought well of his parents back then, they'd only known Brent as the cocky football star. And surely now, with the Woodson name mud, they wouldn't have a good feeling about him.

Barrett took a bite of a mixed-berry scone. "You said Sage's folks are due in town—they moved from Tenacity? Last I remember about Sage Abernathy was that she was a year younger than us and her folks owned a big ranch."

Ah right, Barrett wouldn't even have known that he and Sage had dated. "They left town not long after your family did," Brent explained. "I think they probably thought Tenacity would only go downhill. The plans for the Tenacity Trail were put on hold indefinitely. No money for the fossils dig." Brent sighed. "Not that I want to remember *why*."

Barrett clapped Brent on the shoulder. "I hear ya."

Brent felt funny about mentioning that he and Sage had been a couple back then. That was ancient history. And it seemed clear they wouldn't be getting back together.

"If I'm remembering this right," Barrett said, "Sage had a crush on you in high school. I didn't know her well, but that was the gossip. And you're *extremely* single now, Brent."

Brent had to agree with that. He was very single. And so was Sage. "I don't know. After I ran into her at the inauguration, I asked her to dinner to catch up, and that was last night, but…"

Both men sat up straighter, curiosity plain on their faces.

"But what?" Barrett asked.

"We had a nice dinner at Castillo's, then a nightcap at Grizzly's. I walked her back to the hotel, and that was it. Just catching up—and we did that, so…"

Barrett raised an eyebrow. "So…there's no *but*. Are you gonna ask her out again?"

Brent took a slug of his coffee. "Given everything going on with my family, I don't want to drag her into that by association. Her parents didn't like me fifteen years ago, and they're definitely not gonna like me for their daughter *now*."

"You're in a rough spot," Barrett said with a nod. "But take it from me, don't let the past dictate your present—or future. You're a good guy doing good things. The Abernathys will see that."

Brent took a bite of his blueberry muffin, trying to let his friend and partner's words sink in. To *believe*. "I appreciate the vote of confidence. And having you vouch for me these past six months has done a lot, Barrett. But I don't know. I think Seth is definitely the right guy to approach the Abernathys."

"Get me that contact info as soon as you can," Seth said, "and I'll call them to set up a meeting for when they're in town."

Brent nodded. "I'll do that today." He *did* like having a specific reason to call Sage.

That settled, they moved on to Seth's spreadsheets, talked finances and possibilities, and by the time Seth and Barrett had left, they were all even more sure that the dinosaur park would happen with just a few more investors. That they'd make it happen.

Brent was halfway through another cup of coffee and looking forward to calling Sage when his phone rang. He glanced at it on the table. Sage herself.

He realized he was smiling. "Hey, Sage, nice to hear from you."

"I'm calling for two reasons. First, to thank you for dinner and drinks last night. And second, I'd really like to hear more about plans for the dinosaur park so that I can be in a better position to help convince my parents to invest. They're definitely interested, but since they're spending a small fortune on the new ranch, they'll want more information. They trust me when it comes to finances since that's my role in the family, so if I can help make them more comfortable about the potential, I'd be happy to."

That was a great point about them trusting her when it came to where to spend their money. And if Sage could lay the foundation for why they should invest, Seth Taylor would be in a better position when he met with them.

"If you're free later this afternoon," she said, "we

could meet at the Tenacity Social Club. I used to love that place."

A few memories hit him—in a good way. They'd spent quite a bit of time there during their summer romance. The Tenacity Social Club was a bar at night, and during the day it was a teen hangout—no alcohol, of course, with games, dartboards, old-fashioned pinball machines, and study spaces. There was a long wooden bar where couples would carve their initials. Sage had wanted to do that, and he'd been embarrassed at the time and talked her out of it. He could recall saying, "We're only dating right now" in a harsh kind of a tone. Like they hadn't been a real couple. What a jerk he'd been.

"Sounds great, Sage. And I really appreciate your interest in the park and helping out."

They settled on 4:00 p.m. since Brent had some issues to deal with at the ranch. It took him a moment to hit End Call since he didn't want to break the connection. But he had to think of this as solely a business meeting. Not a date.

For her own good.

It was high time Brent Woodson started doing things that benefitted others even when it hurt him.

The Tenacity Social Club was full of teenagers. Three forty-five—Sage had arrived a little early for her meeting with Brent—was prime time for the place to be a hangout after school. She'd suggested the afternoon to make sure their time together wouldn't feel date-like, as it had last night.

Sage had had a fitful night's sleep, waking up twice—her secret suspicions about who had hidden the money Brent's mother had stolen on her mind. As she'd gotten ready for bed last night, she'd decided to put some distance between her and Brent. What she believed, what she thought had happened back then, didn't matter anymore. Brent's mother had stolen that money—that was not in doubt. And June Woodson wouldn't have been able to run off with her lover anyway, because her husband had found out about the affair and had threatened Barrett Sr. with framing his son for the crime. The Deroys had fled town, mission accomplished.

But Brent did like to talk about the past. He had questions and she was a good listener, someone who'd been around back then who knew the basic details—and then some. How could she continue to get close to him and not tell him what she suspected? She'd had that entire conversation with herself as she'd finally drifted off, fretting.

And then she'd woken up and realized that the past was the past and maybe they all just needed to let it go. That it didn't matter who'd hidden the money under the boulder on the Juniper Road property.

Except maybe it did matter. The fact that the money had disappeared meant that June Woodson, once her plan had been thwarted, couldn't secretly return the money the same way she'd stolen it. She might have been able to give it back on the down-low and the town would have been saved some additional hardships.

If Sage was right about her suspicions. She was pretty sure, but not 100 percent, of course.

And when she'd woken up for good at 6:30 this morning, her brain had settled on *that*—that she wasn't sure and therefore she had to let it go. Her sleep-deprived brain had also settled on the fact that she could do Brent a favor by getting more information about the dinosaur park in order to help sway her difficult parents about investing. Once they knew he was involved, they might lose interest in the project—they *were* that petty. But if she could give them solid facts about the potential for the park, they'd already have that info before they ever knew Brent Woodson was connected to the foundation behind it.

And now they were meeting in fifteen minutes. At a non-date hour. A business meeting, really. She sucked in a breath.

Sage could rationalize this all she wanted, but dammit, she liked Brent. She especially liked the *new* Brent.

Just see, she told herself. *Just give this a chance.*

The *new* Sage was supposed to be going after what she wanted. But what if doing just that blew up on her?

Okay, enough, she told herself. *Just focus on the now.*

She looked around, a smile forming at the groups of teenage girls who were just like she'd been—some studying, some taking selfies, some whispering with friends. Guys playing pinball and arm wrestling. A couple, fifteen or sixteen years old, were sitting on beanbags, holding hands and gazing into each other's eyes. Ah memories. She and Brent had been fond of the beanbags, though Brent had definitely been more interested in the crowd than in her. He'd pop up and go play a round of darts or go join a conversation, his loud laughter carrying and making her feel left out.

Brent Woodson did seem very different now, but Sage had a lot of questions for herself these days, and one of them was why she'd liked a guy who'd treated her the way he had. Maybe back then she'd been too enamored with him to notice or care that he didn't exactly return her feelings. But she'd certainly never been one to stand up for herself, fight for herself, demand her due. Until lately.

But all this did make her wonder if she was repeating old patterns—not seeing who Brent really was. She didn't think that was the case. But she did need to be smart about her heart. Especially when it concerned her first love.

"Sage Abernathy! It *is* you!"

Sage turned from her stool at the bar to find Leigh Wheeler gaping at her and pulling her into a hug. They'd been friends freshman year, but Leigh had ditched Sage in a few months for the popular crowd and never spoke to her again.

Leigh, constantly smoothing her long, light-brown hair and applying lipstick, started talking and didn't stop, catching Sage up on her life despite not having been asked or asking a single question about Sage. Some people definitely didn't change.

"Now, what do I remember about you?" Leigh asked herself. "Let me see. You moved away the summer before sophomore year, I think. And I think you were dating Brent Woodson. All of us were talking about that back then. I mean, you didn't really seem his type. But you got him. Good for you! Of course, no one would be saying 'good for you' now." She turned to wave at someone, a girl around ten or so playing cards at the far end. "That's my gorg niece. I'm picking her up as a favor to my sister. I'm practicing my mom skills now that my hubby and I are trying for a baby."

Sage smiled, feeling a brief sting of envy that she wasn't anywhere close to even being married.

"No ring?" Leigh interrupted, eyeing Sage's bare left hand. "Well, there are a few good single men in Tenacity. Be careful of the players, though. Like your old boyfriend, Brent. I think he's dated *every* woman in town at some point." She rolled her eyes. "Of course, those days are over *now*."

Sage felt herself bristling. What a gossiping snake. "Well, I come to my own conclusions about people based on who they show me they are," she said, feeling her eyes narrowing. *Like you, for instance.*

Leigh face registered her surprise; then she looked past Sage. "Oh, my niece is ready to go." And with that, she hurried off.

Sage shook her head. The new Sage did seem to be making herself known. She smiled, but it faded as Leigh's words came back to her.

Be careful of the players, though. Like your old boyfriend, Brent. I think he's dated every woman in town at some point. Of course, those days are over now.

Mandy might be a viper, but there was probably some truth to what she'd said.

Then again, those days *were* over. This was all new now. And that was what Sage was going to focus on.

"Hey there," came a familiar deep voice.

Sage turned to find Brent approaching.

Her heart gave a little flip, and a bunch of butterflies let loose in her stomach. He wore jeans and a brown leather barn coat, a dark brown Stetson, and cowboy boots. He unzipped his coat, revealing a navy sweater that made his blue eyes even deeper. She was attracted to the man inside and out.

Trouble.

Chapter Five

The sight of Sage at the bar caused tiny explosions like fireworks in Brent's chest. He'd been looking forward to this all day. Earlier that afternoon he'd walked right into the wood fence at the far pasture because he'd been thinking about her. Her face, how sexy she was in her formfitting jeans, the way she looked at him, how immediately they'd fallen back into their old easy fit...

Such anticipation. She wore a long emerald-green sweater with a white camisole peeking out and a few turquoise necklaces of various lengths, dark jeans, and her cowboy boots. Her hair was in a low ponytail, showing off her creamy neck. Her smile lit up her beautiful face.

A familiar country song started playing, and a booming voice came over the mic. "Teens, you've got one more hour to enjoy your time at the Tenacity Social Club, so how about some line dancing!"

Brent could see the daytime manager of the club at the DJ station, which involved a back corner table, his phone, and a Bluetooth speaker. A bunch of people, from teenagers to adults, cheered and wolf-whistled as they made a beeline to the dance floor.

Brent had never been much of a dancer, but he sure wouldn't mind having Sage in his arms—not that line dancing would accomplish that. He'd have to wait for a slow song, which was unlikely at the club during the day, since no one wanted to encourage that kind of close contact among hormonal teens. He smiled to himself, remembering how he and Sage would sometimes dance chest to chest anyway during even fast songs.

Since Sage already had a club soda, Brent got himself a Coke. "Should we grab some chairs, or would you like to stay here?" he asked, shrugging out of his coat.

"I see two comfy chairs over there," she said, pointing. "And we'd have a great view of the dance floor. I love watching people dance."

"I remember how much you liked dancing," he said as she stood up and grabbed her coat.

"Still do," she said as they headed over to the two overstuffed mismatched chairs and sat down. They watched the dance floor a moment; then she turned to him and said, "So I'd love to hear more about the dinosaur park. Anything that would help me talk it up to my parents."

He could feel his excitement, hear it in his voice as he told Sage about two sets of dinosaur bones being found recently in Tenacity—in the woods and in a big open field where the town had held a "pumpkin chunkin" contest last October. How that had led Seth Taylor to bring paleontologist Andrea Spence on board to confirm the finds. Sage's eyes lit up at Seth's name, and she mentioned the family connection, so Brent told her that Seth planned to call her to get her parents' contact info.

They mused about what a small world it was, and then Brent got back to the park itself, how they all believed that with the right equipment, even more fossils would be found in the town.

"We envision a major tourist attraction in Tenacity—a museum having the fossils on display, kids' activities, and life-size models of various dinosaurs." He pulled out his phone and clicked open Seth's spreadsheet. Because of the tiny print, he scooted closer, as did Sage, so close that he could smell her intoxicating perfume. He needed to concentrate on their conversation more than on how close her lips were. Kissing distance. A turn to the right would be all it took.

Focus, he told himself, forcing his eyes off her face and onto his phone. He showed Sage the figures of how much the foundation had already taken in, an analysis of costs for the dig and creation of the park, and projections for revenue once the park was up and running.

"Wow, very impressive," she said, her brown eyes twinkling with excitement. "I'll easily be able to talk up the foundation and the park to my parents. I think they'd be proud to invest. They'll definitely want to talk to Seth when they get to town in a couple days."

"Perfect—and thanks," he said, finishing his soda. Suddenly, he wished he had more left so there would be reason to stay. They were all set about the park. Their glasses were empty. But once again, Brent was not ready to leave, not ready to say goodbye to Sage.

"You know what I could go for?" Sage asked, smiling. "An orange soda. One of my favorite things about the Tenacity Social Club was that you could always get an orange soda."

He felt his smile stretch ear to ear—they were not leaving. *Thank you, orange soda.* "I'd love some too." They headed up to the bar and ordered. Brent wasn't familiar with the woman behind the bar. He did know the other bartender, Mike Cooper, who was engaged to Seth Taylor's brother, Daniel. Even when the news had come out about Brent's family and he'd shied away from his old haunts, he'd run into Mike, who'd said, *Haven't seen you around, Brent—come on by soon for a beer on me.* He'd never forgotten that kindness.

They stood at the bar and sipped their sodas, Brent barely able to take his eyes off Sage. How had he possibly been so cavalier about her fifteen years ago? It was hard to imagine now. She'd been his girlfriend. He'd had *everything* then and hadn't known it.

Nope, wait, he reminded himself. *You didn't have everything. You had no idea what was going on in your own home. With both your parents.*

He'd known they constantly bickered, but just thought it was what parents did. *You were clueless in the worst way.*

Luckily, Sage's beautiful smile pulled him out of his glum thoughts. Suddenly, she extended her hand. "I think it's time we danced," she said.

If only she'd said *kissed*… "Uh, you do remember I'm a terrible dancer. Zero rhythm."

She laughed. "Line dancing just requires you to

move your feet. Just watch the line in front of you and follow along, and you'll do great."

He doubted that, but he was game. He also knew it was the tail end of the song and he'd only have to suffer embarrassment for his bad moves for about thirty seconds.

Because this was the last song for the teenagers, the kids were living it up on the dance floor, moving with gusto and singing at the tops of their lungs. It was impossible not to be drawn in by their enthusiasm, and both he and Sage were singing, too, swaying their hips as they shuffled their feet.

"This is pure fun," he shouted over the music and singing teens. "I didn't even know I needed this."

Sage laughed. "Same."

And suddenly, way too soon, the song was over, and the manager was telling the teens to pack up and make sure they had all their stuff. Brent and Sage watched them all flurry around, and when the last of them trickled out the door, he was sorry to see them go. He and Sage got their orange sodas from the bar and made their way back to their overstuffed chairs.

"Pumpkin hour," Sage said, plopping down. "Well, sort of. When the Tenacity Social Club turns from teen hangout to adult bar."

"I used to love coming here with you," he said, feeling so nostalgic. Back then, he'd had no idea that one day, his family would fall apart. The Woodson name would be mud. His reputation in tatters. His entire life needing a serious do-over. Ignorance was definitely not bliss, but back then, his biggest problem was that the girl he had a crush on didn't return his feelings.

And the woman sitting beside him in the overstuffed chair right now had been beside him then, but he'd been too dumb to realize how great she was. Great in general and great for *him*.

"I wish I'd handled things differently fifteen years ago," he said. "I wished I'd *been* different. The kind of guy your parents would have thought was a good boyfriend. Instead, they probably sold their ranch and moved just to get you away from me."

"Hey, let's not go *that* far. You weren't the reason they wanted to leave Tenacity. They just wanted to try life in Cheyenne, a place with more going on, more prosperity. And the fact that a very popular jock couldn't see me might have made moving seem even better. But there are popular jocks everywhere."

Was that a little stab of jealousy he felt? "Did you date another football player when you moved to Cheyenne?" He suddenly wanted to know about her past relationships. Then again, maybe he didn't.

She gave him a shy smile. "Hardly, Brent. I was pretty brokenhearted about our breakup."

He winced. He hated that he'd hurt her. "If I could go back, I'd know what I had in you. When you told me we had to break up, I should have knocked on your parents' door, convinced them with all I had in me that I'd respect their daughter in all ways and treat her like the treasure she is."

Sage touched her hand to her heart. "That's nice to hear, Brent. I have to say, you did hurt my feelings when you weren't interested in carving our initials on the bar top," she added, gesturing toward the long wooden bar behind them. "Like Barrett and Nina did."

Brent gave a slow shake of his head, recalling seeing their initials back then and wanting to carve through the *B&N4EVER*. "*What* was wrong with me? I'm sorry about that, Sage."

"You were getting over another girl," she said. "I probably should have stepped away, knowing full well you were rebounding."

"Hey, don't put that on you. I shouldn't have dated you in the first place if I couldn't be a good boyfriend."

"Well, then we wouldn't have our history," Sage said. "It might not be perfect, but it's ours."

Brent felt warmth flood his chest. He didn't deserve Sage then, but he hoped he deserved her now. If there *would be* a now. Without thinking, he took her hand and held it. "That, I agree with one hundred percent."

She leaned a bit closer. "Then maybe we should take this second chance to get it right."

His heart did a backflip of happiness. For a moment, he just let her words sink in. But they needed to be realistic. "I want that, Sage. I really do. But you should stay far away from the Woodson mess. You've seen the glares, heard the whispers. Things have gotten better for me, yes, but I'm still a long way from being accepted. Any association with me will just drag you down, and you just got to town."

"Want to know what I think about all that?" she asked.

He wasn't sure he did. What if she agreed with him? Which she should—for her own well-being. "Yes."

She leaned even closer. Closer. And then put her hands on either side of face—and kissed him.

Gently. Then with a little passion.

Every nerve ending in his body tingled.

She pulled back just slightly, and he missed the feel of her lips on his immediately. "I'm my own woman now. I don't give a rat's earlobe what anyone thinks except for you and me."

For a moment, he couldn't respond—that was how moved he was. "You're something else, Sage Abernathy."

"I hope so," she said.

He laughed and gazed at her beautiful face. "Is that a saying, a rat's earlobe?"

"I don't know," she said. "I just made it up. But it should be a saying."

He smiled and touched her cheek and then leaned in for another kiss. Warm. Soft. Passionate.

He was taking this second chance. And vowed right here and now to be very careful with it.

Chapter Six

At close to seven that night, Sage stood at the stove in Brent's kitchen, adding fettuccini to the big pot of boiling water. As they'd been leaving the Tenacity Social Club a couple of hours ago, Brent had suggested they celebrate their second chance with dinner at a romantic restaurant in a bigger town a half hour away. But Sage had had an even better idea: She wanted to cook for him at his house. He'd instantly agreed that would be more romantic—but only if he could help. Which made the idea a million times more romantic for her.

He'd given her one hell of a kiss goodbye outside the club, and when Sage had opened her eyes, her knees slightly wobbly and her toes tingling, she'd noticed a few people eyeing them. *Let 'em look*, she'd thought. She and Brent were going to be dating, so there was no time like that very second to get used to being stared at and whispered about.

They'd decided on 7:00 p.m. at the ranch, and she'd floated off to the Tenacity Grocery to pick up the ingredients for dinner. Fettuccini carbonara, Italian bread, and cheesecake for dessert. She couldn't remember the last time she'd been that excited about a date, about the possibilities. So much so that she put her worries aside. The ones about the secrets she'd kept from Brent back then—and now. As she'd been grabbing a half-dozen eggs, a little voice had said, *Put all that out of your head for now. You don't even know if your suspicions are true. Just focus on the two of you. See what's there. You'll know when it's time for your concerns to come out.*

And so she'd hurried home, taken a luxurious shower, smoothed on scented body lotion, and had taken a lot more time with her appearance than she normally did. She'd packed one dress, a simple black jersey wrap-style that could be dialed down or dolled up, and she'd gone for casual. For jewelry, just her everyday tiny heart pendant that her late maternal grandmother had given her when she was sixteen. She'd kept her makeup light. But she did go for her knee-high boots.

And the way Brent had looked at her when she arrived at his house and had helped her off with her coat had told her the outfit had done its job. *This* was a date. And a special one—commemorating their second chance. A new start.

He'd surprised her with a beautiful bouquet of flowers, which now were in a vase on the kitchen table. And he'd set out a bottle of wine and two glasses. They sipped as they got started on cooking dinner.

"Put me to work," Brent said, coming up behind her and putting his hands on her shoulders. He was practically pressing against her. He smelled so good. A combination of clean soap and fresh shampoo and delicious aftershave.

Her nerve endings tingled again.

She set the stove timer for nine minutes for the pasta. "You can crack two eggs into a bowl and add two egg yolks while I get busy with the bacon."

"I'm on it," he said, reaching up into the cabinet for a bowl.

He smiled so warmly at her that her heart was close to bursting. This was what she'd been longing for with a man, this kind of happy, fun domesticity on a date. That she was having this experience with her first love fifteen years later was like a dream. She'd taken off her boots at the door when she'd first arrived, and they were both barefoot, making this feel even cozier somehow.

The delicious aroma of sizzling bacon filled the kitchen. She gave Brent the task of adding the cheeses to the eggs, and he was whisking away.

"Are you much of a cook?" she asked.

"I've become one out of need. Until six months ago, I was out and about all the time. Always at the Grizzly or grabbing breakfast and lunch at the Silver Spur. But then I quickly realized I needed to lay low, so I had to learn how to cook. I googled recipes, and after a lot of trial and error, I'm okay at the basics."

She pictured Brent alone in his kitchen, sad and hurting, hunched over a recipe on his phone, chopping vegetables or waiting for a burger to brown. "Aw. Are your favorites still the same as when you were sixteen? Cheeseburgers, pizza, mac and cheese?"

He laughed. "I like everything now. But I make a lot of steak and potatoes. I'm not bad at Western omelets.

MELISSA SENATE   83

I still can't make a decent smoothie, though. I either add too little this or too much that."

Sage smiled. "I'll make you one of my creations some time." *Maybe tomorrow morning*, she thought with a naughty inner glow. She had no idea where this date would go, but *she'd* go where it led—whatever felt right.

"So you haven't done much dating the past six months?" she asked, with some hesitation in her voice because she figured it was the case. Those two women she'd run into had pretty much said he'd been a player until he couldn't be. That had given her pause. If Brent Woodson's life hadn't exploded, would he still be dating every woman in Tenacity? Would he even be interested in his old summer girlfriend?

Don't go there, she told herself. *None of that matters. His life did explode, and he changed because of it. There was before and there's now. Now is all you need to focus on.*

"When the truth came out about my parents," he said, "I was dating two women casually and—"

"And when you say *casually*," she interrupted, "do you mean sleeping with them?"

His cheeks flushed, which she thought was sweet. A question like that probably wouldn't have affected the old Brent. "No. Both were new. Second date with one and a couple of weeks with the other. Lots of making out, but that was it. But when word spread about what my parents had done, they dumped me before *I* could even tell them what happened."

"Sorry," she said, her heart aching for him. His

whole life really had been turned upside down with people assuming the worst about him. That had to be very painful to endure.

"It was rough at first because I was used to things being a certain way. Easy. Pretty much dating who-ever I thought was hot. And when it was cut off, when everything changed, *hot* was the last thing I was in-terested in. For the first time, other traits became very important to me. Like someone who doesn't rush to judgment. Someone who's understanding. Compas-sionate. A good listener. Insightful. If she happens to be absolutely breathtaking, with driftwood-brown eyes and long, swirly blond hair—well, that's nice too."

Her heart gave a leap. "I'm glad you see me that way, Brent. I mean—the important traits. That means a lot to me."

He turned and touched her chin. "I can't believe I had you right beside me fifteen years ago and took you for granted. What an idiot I was. I can promise you that will never happen again. I know how lucky I am that you're giving me this second chance."

She put down her wooden spoon and pulled him into a kiss, which got as steamy as the kitchen. It was good that the oven timer dinged, or they might have both ripped off their clothes right there and then.

"We can save that very good thought for later," he said with a sexy smile. She had him drain the pasta and pour it from the colander into the pan; then she added the eggs and cheese mixture and gave it all a stir. "That looks and smells amazing. Kind of like you."

"You can compare my scent to fettuccini carbonara anytime," she said with a smile. "It's my favorite dish." He moved behind her and put his arms around her and kissed her cheek, then just held her that way for a moment.

Right now, everything in the world was okay.

"I'm starving," he said. "And I love that we cooked together."

She grinned and cut up the loaf of Italian bread, putting it in a bowl. "Me too. Let's eat."

He set the table, lighting a candle near the flowers. Then he topped off their glasses. With the fireplace crackling across in the living room and some low music playing from a Bluetooth speaker, this dinner was as romantic as they'd both imagined it would be.

They sat down, Brent holding up his glass. "To us. To second chances."

"To second chances," she said, her heart pinging in her chest, as it had been doing for the past forty-five minutes.

They dug in, Brent declaring the pasta the best carbonara he'd ever had. "So tell me about *your* past relationships," he said, swirling a bite on his fork. "What was your last one like?"

Oops. She should have expected he'd ask about her love life since she'd asked about his. And hers had been pretty dull. "The last one, we were dating for two months, seeing each other about three times a week," she said. She sipped her wine. "I was beginning to feel like something was just missing, and was planning on talking to him about that to see if he thought the same. But he ghosted me. Just stopped calling or texting or responding. And then I saw him walking hand in hand with a very attractive redhead. I guess he did feel the way I did—but thanks for letting me know, bub." She shook her head and smiled.

"So rude and disrespectful of that guy. Good riddance."

"Right? And before that, I was in a relationship for over a year and did have feelings for him, but I can't say I ever felt that deep, burning love, you know? The way I've been waiting to feel." *The way I felt about you when I was fifteen years old.* Maybe it had been puppy love, but she hadn't experienced that level of intensity since. "I was getting worried that I'd never feel it. I had a few of those kinds of relationships throughout my twenties."

"Same," he said. "I've had strong feelings, but I'd never felt whatever it is that makes people want to get down on one knee and propose."

It gave her a secret thrill to know that they were aligned in that, that they'd never been in love before as adults. Sage had definitely been excited about some of the men she'd dated, but she'd never felt quite like she felt around Brent—then or now.

They moved on to talking about their favorites, to see what had stood the test of time from when they were teens, from food to movies to music. They had a lot in common, like Mexican food, superhero movies, and the color blue, but he loved horror flicks and she couldn't watch them. She loved taking long drives, but he got car sick. He liked ketchup on hot dogs, but she was strictly mustard. They'd both eaten their fill and carried the dishes into the kitchen, cleaning up together. They kissed as they worked. Sipped their wine. Talked and laughed and flirted.

And then the kitchen was sparkling clean and he suggested they move into the living room. He sat down on the sofa and pulled her onto his lap, which was exactly where she wanted to be.

He kissed her so tenderly, looking at her, touching her face, making her feel so special, so cared for, so desired. "I'm loving this second chance."

"Me too," she said, looking into his eyes. She saw sincerity there. Unmistakable happiness. And desire.

She suddenly felt emboldened. "My favorite thing about this dress is that if you pull the bow, the whole thing just unravels," she whispered into his ear. "Makes it very easy to take off."

Invitation proffered. Initiating to this degree was hardly like her, but being with the man she'd never stopped fantasizing about seemed to bring out a different side of her. A side she liked. Still, was she moving too fast? Maybe. But her heart and head were working together right now. She wanted this. Even if a relationship with Brent didn't work out. She hadn't gotten past kissing him all these years ago. And she'd fantasized plenty about him between then and now. Over the years she'd never stopped thinking about him, wondering how he was, what he was doing, if he missed her at all. Now she had the chance to be with him—and with Brent the *man*.

"That is very good to know," he said, his voice

husky. "I don't mind working hard to get you naked, though."

A thrill ran up her spine. Invitation accepted.

Sage grinned. "Also good to know."

He kissed her so passionately that she inwardly gasped, and she felt his hand going to the bow at her waist. He gave it a tug.

She moved off his lap and stood, facing him, the dress falling open. He took her in, staring—hungrily, she could easily see— at her body. She pushed the material from her shoulders, and the dress fell into a little heap on the rug. Then he slowly tugged her back down so that she was straddling him.

Her body was on fire. Her intake of breath fueled her to lean against him to trail kisses up his neck as she unbuttoned his shirt. Darn it—T-shirt underneath. That had to go fast. She slid her hands underneath the cotton, his skin warm. She could feel his heart pulsating under her touch. She tugged off the button-down and lifted the T-shirt over his head, his glorious rock-hard chest with a smattering of blond hair causing her own breath to quicken. His body had changed. She'd seen him shirtless back then, of course, when they'd gone swimming. He'd had the body of a teen-aged boy—albeit a star football player. Now, he was very much a man.

His hands were all over her—at her waist, up her sides, lingering on the cups of her lacy black bra. He leaned forward to kiss her cleavage, then unhooked the bra and pushed it off her shoulders. His hands were on her breasts, his mouth following, and she arched her back in such pleasure, such anticipation, that a breathy moan escaped her.

"You liked that, did you?" he whispered, kissing her neck, his tongue lightly caressing her ear. One of his hands went to the button of his jeans.

"Let me," she said, glancing up at him before moving off to kneel in front. She slowly slid down the zipper, his intake of breath and the way his body froze letting her know he was trying to control himself. She yanked down his jeans, and he quickly shrugged them off, then pulled her closer, hooking a finger in the side of her black panties and slowly easing them down her thighs until they pooled at her feet.

She slid a hand inside his sexy boxer briefs, and he moaned and leaned his head back; then she slid them down his hips and legs until they joined her own undies.

"The sofa would be very hot," he said. "But I want you in my bed." He shifted and scooped her up, kissing her along the way to his bedroom up the stairs.

He nudged a door farther open with his foot and laid her down on the bed, and all the glorious extra room made exploring each other's bodies much easier. "I'm in heaven," he whispered.

"Me too," she whispered back.

And then he laid fully on top of her, kissing her neck, her collarbone. She writhed in anticipation, about to ask if he had a condom, when she heard the side table drawer open and shut and a foil packet being ripped open.

And as they finally became one, Sage meeting the

intensity, the urgency of his thrusts, the waves of pleasure releasing so much pent-up tension, all Sage could
think was, *I love you. I've always loved you.*

Brent woke up in his dark bedroom, instantly
aware that Sage was sleeping beside him, curled into
his side, her arm across his torso. He pressed a gentle
kiss against her temple and then glanced at his phone
on his bedside table: 1:24 a.m. A bit of moonlight was
shining through the room from the windows, and Brent
could see the stars.

He made a wish: *Let me have this. Don't let this explode in my face like some other things in my life lately.*

He hoped the stars were listening. He needed this,
needed Sage. He wasn't used to that, wasn't quite comfortable with needing someone, but something else was
bigger: his feelings for her. He *liked* this woman. A lot.

And taking her to bed had released so much pent-
up tension in his mind and body, his heart and soul.
He turned slightly to look at her beautiful face, could
see her chest rising and falling with her breaths under
the comforter. He smoothed back a swath of her wavy,
blond hair, the scent of her shampoo bringing back
memories of her hair falling over his face and chest as
they'd made love, Sage on top for a while, Brent trying to keep control so that this night might last forever.

He liked that she was here, sleeping over. At least it
looked that way. He hoped she wouldn't wake up and
get dressed and want to leave. Given how they'd fit
so perfectly together, how they'd drifted off to sleep

spooned, he had the sense the night had been as magical to her as it had been to him.

But as Brent had said, he took nothing for granted. Didn't assume.

She stirred and turned slightly, facing him more fully, and her driftwood-brown eyes opened. What he saw in them brought a smile. She looked very happy.

"Am I dreaming?" she whispered.

"When I woke up a little while ago, I wondered the same."

"Pinch me so I know," she said, holding out her arm.

"Never. I never want to do anything to hurt you again."

Sage smiled and reached a hand out to touch his face. "Want to know something?"

Brent nodded.

"When I came over earlier, I brought my large purse and stuffed it with my toiletries and a change of clothes for tomorrow morning. Just in case. Guess I was on the right track."

He grinned and kissed her. "I could easily never leave this bed. We could order food for days."

"Um, from where?" she asked. "This is Tenacity."

"True, but soon enough, Tenacity will be such a popular tourist destination that new businesses will be opening every day. We'll be able to order sushi at two a.m. if we wanted. There will be five pizzerias, and all will deliver."

Sage laughed. "That would nice. Everyone will love you for it."

He almost blurted out, *Who needs everyone? I just*

need you. And good thing he didn't. Because a slight chill ran up his spine. He was getting way ahead of himself.

"Including my parents," she said. "They're arriving the day after tomorrow. I'm excited for them to have a chance to get to know the man you are today."

A second chill crawled across the nape of his neck. "Sage, I don't want you get your hopes up. Once your folks hear about what my parents did to Barrett…"

She smoothed back the hair at his temple. "They'll know that people have been very unfair to you. That you were sixteen years old. That you didn't know a thing about what your mom and dad were each doing. That now you're taking time away from your ranch to put your heart and soul into the foundation to revital-ize Tenacity—I mean, that will count a lot. They're moving here."

Her faith in him meant so much, but he just had a bad feeling about this. She had such a combination of hope and surety in her eyes, in her voice, that he knew to let it go. She could be right about her parents—she certainly knew them when he didn't at all beyond what she'd talked about fifteen years ago. That they were interested in investing in the dinosaur park said a lot about them—that they cared about Tenacity, that they saw the potential the same way he did.

"Maybe you're right," he said. "I have a special in-terest in making a good impression on them." He kissed her on the nose, on the forehead, and ran a finger down her cheek. "One that has nothing to do with investing in the dinosaur park."

Her smile went straight into his heart. "Let's trust in what can be," she said. "That's my new motto."

Trust in what can be. He silently repeated it. "I'm sold." He could feel the tension leaving his body. Sage Abernathy was good for him in so many ways. "I wish I could spend the morning with you, but I promised my neighbor I'd help him with some problems at his ranch at nine. I'll have to say goodbye to you around eight forty-five."

"What? No morning sex?" she said with a grin.

"Hey, it's morning *now*. Wee hours."

She moved on top of him, taking his hands and pushing them over his head up onto the pillow, then kissed him passionately, making him throb with need and anticipation. He ran his hands down her body and made a vow that no matter what happened he'd fight for this.

Because Sage Abernathy was the best thing that had happened to him in a long time.

Chapter Seven

Later that morning, Sage was so in her head—in a good way—that she got honked at after not paying attention as she crossed Central Avenue. But nothing could touch her great mood. Her body had never felt so loose and limber, not even after the hot yoga she'd tried last year. Her date with Brent had been magical, from the moment she'd arrived until she'd left his ranch a couple of hours ago.

It had been so hard to leave. They'd made love again, then had taken a shower together with a lot of kissing under the rain head. He'd insisted on making her breakfast—and not a quick bowl of cereal. He'd whipped up bacon-and-cheese omelets and buttered sourdough toast with honey, a bowl of strawberries, and of course, coffee. Then, with a kiss, he'd had to say goodbye and they'd parted ways—but not until making plans to get together later this afternoon.

Sage couldn't wait.

Not that she didn't have some questions for herself, but they could all wait. Right now, she just wanted to luxuriate in how wonderful she felt. After all, her parents were arriving tomorrow and she'd have to come to a decision about her life, because if she wasn't moving to Tenacity with them to handle the new ranch's finances, they'd have to hire someone else. Or take over the job themselves. Her dad was great with numbers and very responsible, and lately he'd been scaling back some of the more physical ranch duties, hiring two extra hands. He could easily take on the books and would enjoy that role.

And she could pursue her dream to paint. Here in Tenacity, where her new love was? If she could focus on her art—with the man she was falling in love with *and* her family nearby—she was all for it.

Her plan right now was to get herself another cup of coffee from the Silver Spur, then sit down at the counter with her phone to research potential studios she might rent in town. She knew that Tenacity had apartments for rent, but perhaps there were some old storefronts she could turn into an art studio for herself. She just needed good light and her supplies. Her mind or photographs would fill in for what the immediate landscape didn't. So even a workspace on Central Avenue would be just fine.

The more she thought about it, the more excited she got.

The wind picked up, and she walked up the street toward the Silver Spur Café, and she wrapped her scarf more tightly around her neck, wishing she had Brent's warm arms around her.

"Hey, Sage!"

She turned to find three women—her old friends from Tenacity High—coming up the sidewalk. Lily,

Elena, and Keisha. Her heart leaped at the sight of them, even though they hadn't kept in touch for long after she'd moved. They'd been her group. They'd texted and video-called constantly the first few weeks, but after a couple of months with her way out in Cheyenne, the communication had petered out. She'd figured she wasn't part of their world anymore, and so they'd reached out less and less to share or get her take on things. She'd been so hurt at the time. And strangely, it had been her mom who'd had some words of wisdom.

Honey, people will always come in and out of your life, even friends you were close to. It doesn't mean they weren't real friends. Some things just become situational. It's just how life is. Ebbs and flows. You'll make new friends here in Cheyenne, you'll see.

Sage had made new friends, even a bestie named Jodie, but she'd found herself holding back from most people and never got as close as she'd been with Lily, Elena, and Keisha. She'd been described as aloof a few times, which had stung, but she supposed it was a defense mechanism. She'd never meant to keep herself at a distance from people, but she must have always done it without realizing. Hard as it could be, the new Sage would try to let people get close.

The way she was doing with Brent. Then again, that seemed to be happening of her heart's own accord, her head just slightly behind.

The three women hugged her and they briefly caught up—all three were married, and Elena had two children, whereas both Lily and Keisha were actively trying for a baby. Sage reported she was still single, and she did notice that usual slight look of pity on their faces. Or maybe Sage was just being sensitive. Sometimes it seemed everyone was married but her. And she was *thirty* now.

"It's cold out," Lily said, rubbing her gloved hands together. "Catch up inside?"

Sage hesitated. She didn't really know these three anymore, but their expressions were open and friendly, so she decided why not; she'd been wanting to get coffee anyway. After the last two people she'd run into, who'd only had negative things to say about Brent, she didn't want anyone talking against him. Would her old group of friends be different?

They went inside and ordered at the counter—a basic hazelnut drip coffee for Sage—then sat down at a back table.

"Sooo," Elena said, then took a sip of her coffee. "We were hoping we'd run into you! I told these two I could have sworn I saw you going into Castillo's with Brent Woodson the other night. It *was* you!"

"Does this mean you two are dating again?" Keisha asked, breaking off a piece of her scone.

They all leaned closer. Tenacity was a small town, and everyone noticed everything. Especially when it came to Brent.

Sage tried to keep her expression neutral. "We ran into each other at the mayoral inauguration for the first time in fifteen years." There was no way she could keep her happiness off her face. She could feel herself beaming. "We're seeing each other again."

The women's faces all lit up. "That's so romantic,"

Keisha said, tossing her long, curly brown hair behind her shoulder. "I remember that you were completely crazy about him, but then you had to move."

"It's so interesting to date my first love," Sage said. "And I say *first love* kind of loosely, I guess, since we only were a couple for part of a summer and just kissed." This was nice, talking this way with girl-friends. Hanging out with these three felt like old times. Maybe if she did stay in town, they could pick up their friendship where they'd left off—as if hardly any time had passed. It almost felt like that.

"I love it," Lily said, her hazel eyes sparkling. "I'm Team Brent all the way. And trust me, I remember him as an arrogant loudmouth big man on campus. But I've seen him fighting for Tenacity's future these past six months. His speech at the inauguration was really impressive."

Sage felt herself puff up at the praise for Brent. *Damn right*, she wanted to say.

Elena frowned. "Eh. I think he's saying whatever he has to to get back in the public's good graces. I wouldn't be surprised if he's planning to run for mayor next term—easy way to get his standing back."

Uh, no. Definitely not. Brent had his hands full with his ranch and the foundation. And being mayor hadn't gotten his father anywhere when the truth had come out—he'd had to resign in disgrace.

"I don't know," Keisha said after taking a sip of her latte. "I dated a friend of his in high school, and Brent was a good buddy. He tutored the guy in math so he wouldn't get kicked off the football team. And he stopped some of their group from bullying a nerdy kid—I saw that happen myself."

That was nice to hear. She could definitely see the Brent she'd known fifteen years ago being a good friend. She knew he had a blustering side to him too. But he'd always had goodness in his heart.

Lily was nodding. "One time I saw him and his little sister all dressed up in town, and it started pouring. He held his Tenacity High Football umbrella over her head while he got soaked. I never forgot it. I'd always thought he could be a jerk, but the way he treated his sister told me everything I needed to know about Brent Woodson."

Aw. Sage knew how close Brent and Victoria had always been. She could absolutely see him doing that.

"I feel for him," Lily added. "No one knows what to think about what happened fifteen years ago—if Brent *did* know that his dad basically blackmailed the Deroys into leaving town."

"Do you know if he knew?" Keisha asked Sage.

They all leaned close again, three sets of eyes peering at her. Waiting to hear what she knew.

"He didn't know," Sage said with conviction. "I believe that one hundred percent. You can't imagine how painful this has been for him. I mean, not only dealing with the very hard truth about his parents, but with people thinking the worst about him."

The three women seemed to be taking that in, and it seemed clear they hadn't looked at it that way before. If gossip *had* to spread—and it always would, and did— she wouldn't mind for them to share *that* part of it.

Lily nodded thoughtfully. "Well, like I said, I'm Team Brent. My husband and I are just getting by these days, but I donated twenty-five bucks to Brent and Barrett's foundation. I love what they're doing. A dinosaur park will really change things around here."

Elena smiled. "That's so true. It makes me really excited for my kid's future. Tenacity could be very different than the town we grew up in. And that's thanks in part to Brent Woodson, so given what you've all said about him just now, I take back what I said about his motives."

Sage was very happy to hear that. *That* reaction, all their takes, gave her hope about how her parents would feel once they arrived and heard all the gossip about the Woodsons. Rosemary and Bert Abernathy could be very hard on people. Hearing about June Woodson's affair alone could turn off her parents from donating to the foundation. Add in Clifford Woodson blackmailing his wife's lover and casting the blame on his teenage son... Then throw in the Woodson's son "obviously being in on it all along," the very same son who'd been dating their fifteen-year-old daughter and... Sage was worried. Her parents could be self-righteous, accusatory, and judgmental, and they sometimes looked down their noses. Sage loved her parents, and they had wonderful qualities, too, but compassion wasn't among them. They were straight shooters who felt how they felt and went with it.

The foundation, especially with Seth Taylor—his sister married to an Abernathy, even from a different branch—on board, spoke for itself. Sage just hoped her parents would listen to *that*—not the noise.

"One thing is clear to me," Keisha said. "That you're still hung up on Brent. Am I right?"

She was definitely hung up on him. Beyond that, she didn't know. It was very early on in their reunion. She was developing feelings for him—that was undeniable. "He's always had a hold on me," Sage said. "There's just something special between us. Was back then and it's even bigger and brighter now."

"So romantic," Elena said, picking up her coffee. "I'm happy for the two of you."

"I'll put money on you two getting engaged by Valentine's Day," Lily said. "Ladies, mark my words."

Sage had to laugh. "That's next month. We're brand new."

"But *old loves*," Keisha said. "That counts for a lot."

Happy chills ran up Sage's spine. She sat back and sipped her coffee, wondering just what would happen between her and Brent. It would be nice to daydream about a Valentine's Day engagement, fast as that seemed.

But with the secret Sage was carrying around about Brent's family, there would be no real moving forward. A couple couldn't have secrets between them. At some point, she would have to tell him what she knew. Or thought she knew.

And Sage had no doubt it could possibly tear her and Brent apart forever.

A picnic in January in Montana might sound strange, but today's high temperature was an unusual forty-one degrees, with bright sunshine and no wind, and Brent planned to take full advantage of it for his afternoon date with Sage. There was a sturdy lean-to a half mile out on his property that faced a stone firepit, both of which looked more romantic than they sounded—which was why he'd only told Sage he had a little surprise for her and to dress warmly.

He'd pre-stocked the shelter with cozy blankets, pillows, and a picnic basket. There were two Adirondack chairs with cushions around the firepit. His Bluetooth speaker would be at the ready to play soft music. The picnic basket was full of goodies, from sliced meats and cheeses to French bread and fruits and chocolate. And a bottle of wine. All around, there was nothing but land, sky, and the mountain range as far as the eye could see. He had a feeling the landscape would appeal to Sage's inner artist.

He'd picked her up at the Tenacity Inn, and as they'd driven back to his ranch, he couldn't stop replaying moments from last night—moments in bed, and in the shower that morning. But it wasn't just the amazing sex and her naked body on his mind. He'd been able to feel her support, her belief in him. Last night, as he'd let himself be open and vulnerable, he'd never once felt cornered or the need to run—as he'd had with many other encounters.

Let's trust in what can be, she'd said. He was going to work hard to adopt that as his motto too. *What can be* was all he had.

Now, as they walked toward the area, Sage looked all around. "I'm seriously liking this surprise so far.

Why can I breathe better here than on my parents'
ranch in Cheyenne? Same fresh air. Similar vista. How
can it be so much more peaceful here?"

"I think it's all the issues that come with your family's ranch," he said. "The ties that bind."

She nodded. "I've been thinking a lot about that. I
do like those ties. I *want* a close relationship with my
parents, even though they're not easy. But I also want
to be me. The real me." She bit her lip and looked away.
"I'm naive to think I'm close with them if they have no
idea how I really feel. Since I was a kid." She kicked
at a pebble. "Why did I do this to myself? Why didn't
I speak up? You did with your parents. And here you
are—" She waved her hand out at the land, and he
could tell she was on the verge of tears.

"Hey," he said gently, taking her hand. "Everyone
is wired differently. Some people just aren't comfortable rocking the boat, especially with very important
relationships like family. And you had that ingrained in
you from the time you were very small, Sage. You grew
up holding back. Don't be hard on yourself. You're
working through it all now."

She brightened some. "I am, that's true."

He wasn't sure how much to probe about her in-
tentions for herself. He didn't want her to make any
decisions about her life because they were dating. If Tenacity wasn't where she could see herself as a painter,
then she should move to where she could soar. Even if
that left him behind.

Damn, the old Brent Woodson would never have
had a thought like that.

"Are you thinking more about going your own way?" he asked. "Striking out on your own?"

"I want to. But why does it seem so scary? Oh wait, I know why. Because I'm a chicken."

"Nope," Brent said. "It's not like you threw away your paints and brushes," he reminded her. "You've even sold some pieces, right? You've been working on your art all along—in your own way, your own time. Maybe the right time just hadn't presented itself. Until now, with your parents' move."

She turned to him, the sparkle back in her eyes. "You're absolutely right. I have a lot to think about." She lifted her face to the sky and took a deep breath. "Ahhh, this place is so rejuvenating. I should tell you— if you're out with the cattle on some random day or riding fence and see me walking around, it's because I snuck in to do my deep thinking here."

He grinned. "You are welcome to come walking and thinking whenever you want."

She stopped and wrapped him in a hug. He could barely feel her through their winter coats, but he still felt the contact in every nerve ending. "Thanks, Brent. A lot."

He was so moved by how pleased she seemed that he couldn't speak for a second, and so he tipped his hat at her. "I'll tell you something," he said as they resumed walking, "during the darkest times last summer and fall, when I felt so lost, I'd walk my property, I'd tend the cattle, I'd slip my horse a few treats, and I'd come out here—" he pointed ahead to where the lean-to and firepit and chairs could be seen "—and I'd sit for hours and feel okay again. Just like you were describing. I'd have the feeling that deep down, I *do* know who I am. I'd look around the ranch, and that reminded me of what was important to me, what was never-changing, what was everlasting."

She grabbed his hand and held it tightly in her mittened one. "I love that, Brent. That's how painting has always made me feel."

"Please remember you said that, okay?" he asked as they approached the two chairs facing the firepit, the lean-to on the other side. "And now, for your little surprise. A winter picnic. I was paying attention last night when you were telling me your favorite foods."

She laughed, taking it all in. "I love this. Thank you."

"And in there, you'll find blankets and pillows and the picnic basket. But let me get the fire going first."

As Sage sat down in one of the red wooden Adirondack chairs, Brent got busy on the fire, which was soon crackling and warming the air around them. Then he got the picnic basket and a blanket, and when they were seated side by side, he settled the blanket over them.

"This couldn't be more romantic," she said as he uncorked the wine. "And I don't think I could be happier right now."

He held her gaze and leaned to the left to kiss her, his heart racing at how she closed her eyes, her face full of anticipation. "Me too."

Brent opened the wine and poured, holding his glass up.

"I'll make the toast," she said.

He waited, his heart so full he didn't think there was any room for more happiness.

"To us," she said. "Simple but just right."

"Agreed," he said, and they clinked glasses and took a sip, then dug into the basket. He fed her a strawberry; she fed him a grape. He could do that all day, all night, even if it were freezing cold.

"Let me ask you something," she said. She put down her sandwich. "I guess this is on my mind because I'll be seeing my parents tomorrow. I'm wondering where things stand with *your* parents. How is your relationship with your mom and dad?"

"Not great," he said, his chest feeling tight.

"Is it hard to talk about?" she asked.

"Yes, but it's important to talk about it. There are things I haven't really dealt with." He shifted in the chair, staring at the orange flames.

"Like?" she asked.

"Like you said earlier, about questioning things about yourself—I've been doing a lot of that. Why did I just accept my dad's shifty ways my whole life? There was this tacit understanding in the house that sometimes you had to do slightly unethical things for the greater good. Why did I just accept that? Why didn't I push back? You want to know what my answer was? Because I'm a bad person. And that was hard."

"You were never a bad person, Brent. You just told me that I accepted my parents making life decisions for me because it was ingrained in me since I was very young. 'This is how it's gonna be.' Same for you."

He considered that. Her words definitely made him

feel better about it. Until he thought about how far his dad had gone. "I just never could have imagined my father would go so low as to frame an innocent teenage boy for theft to punish my mother for her infidelity." He cringed. "And that was another thing. My mother had an affair? For months? With an old love she'd never gotten over?" He dropped his head back. "Actually, that part makes it even sadder because now I know how strong that kind of connection can be."

Sage reached for his hand and held it. "I'm so sorry, Brent."

"I hate that my mother had an affair, that she was in love with someone else, that she was so miserable she resorted to theft—and to the plan of running away." He shook his head and then got up and faced toward the mountains, his heart heavy.

He could tell Sage had gotten up and was moving next to him. She slung an arm around his shoulder. She wrapped her arms around him, and he held her as the brisk air, the sunshine, and the feel of her against him, her hands on his shoulders, worked their magic. "I'm okay, Sage."

"You don't have to be," she said.

"Took me a while to accept that too. That there will be days even still where all this crap just builds up and I can't believe any of it. I mean, I always knew my parents were far from perfect, that they argued a lot. But they must have been miserable for years. My mom was in love with Barrett Sr. when she married my father. That's crazy."

He filled her in on what he knew, that June and Bar-

rett Sr. had been teenage sweethearts and that Barrett
Sr. had known her parents would never approve of a
guy from a poor family marrying their daughter. So
he'd left town to try to make his name and a fortune on
the rodeo circuit. By the time he got back to town, expecting June to have waited, she'd fallen for someone
else—Clifford Woodson—and married him. So Barrett
had married someone else, and they got on with their
lives, but they'd been drawn back together. Barrett Jr.
had told him all that—he'd heard it straight from his
father—and so had his mother. Both had also told him
that his mother had taken the money to have the funds
to pay for a divorce attorney who would help her get at
least joint custody of Brent and Victoria.

"Good God, Brent," Sage said.

He took her hand and led her back to the chairs,
where they sipped their wine and just stared at the fire
for a little while.

"Are all marriages a lie?" he asked. He let out a
breath. "I know they're not. I've seen good marriages
all over Tenacity. I just know two up close that were
shams."

"Your parents' and the Deroys', you mean? Are the
Deroys going to divorce?"

He nodded. "Barrett said it's already in process.
Same with mine. They still live together in the family
house, though, since they decided not to sell until the
divorce was final. Victoria moved out last summer, but
she said they'd been in separate bedrooms for years
anyway and had taken to shouting at each other from
across the hall."

Sage was quiet for a moment. "There *are* good marriages. My parents individually aren't easy people, but they work together in all ways. They love each other, they're there for each other. My aunts and uncles, grandparents, lots of cousins. So many long and happy marriages. So many *new* marriages because of it."

He nodded and squeezed her hand. "Good. Gives me hope that this very good thing we've started won't end in some garbage heap."

Sage bit her lip and turned to look toward the mountains, and he wondered what she was thinking.

"Did I go too far with the 'garbage heap'?" he asked, trying for a bit of a smile.

"I just really, really care about you, Brent Woodson. And what we have is really special."

"Ditto from me," he said, looking at her and reaching a hand to smooth back her hair where a swath had fallen in her face.

Sage seemed a million miles away all of a sudden. It reminded him that she was a separate person with her own thoughts and take on things. Her own goals and dreams. And that, at any minute, this could fall apart.

Everything in his life these past six months felt like a lie. Maybe he was being a fool to trust in this beautiful thing blooming between them. Was he being naive like he'd been his entire life?

He didn't have the bandwidth to deal with getting blindsided again or feeling any more heartache. Maybe he should take a step back. It was probably a good thing that he couldn't see Sage tonight—he'd promised his neighbor, the rancher he'd helped out this morning, that he'd take an overnight shift watching his sick horse, who required meds and twenty-four-hour care right now.

Besides, Sage's parents were arriving in town tomorrow morning, and it would take about ten minutes for the awful truth about what his parents had done, what the Woodson name had turned into in Tenacity, to reach their ears. The Abernathys might not even want to move here, let alone invest in the dinosaur park.

But as he looked at Sage, beautiful Sage, sitting beside him, he realized he needed to stop thinking about himself and start thinking about *her*. She didn't look very happy anymore, and he wanted to turn that around.

"I guess this got heavy for a picnic," he said.

"Well, it is a *winter* picnic."

He laughed and held up his glass, and they clinked again. "All I know for absolute sure in this world, Sage Abernathy, is that I'm glad I'm here with you."

"Me too," she said, linking her arm around his. "Me too."

And with that, he settled back in his chair, back in the picnic, and breathed a little easier. Tomorrow might be another story, but right now, they were here, and he was going to make the most of what could get complicated fast.

Chapter Eight

The Tenacity Inn did not have a penthouse suite—the hotel wasn't remotely that kind of place—but Sage's parents kept referring to their room that way because it was on the top floor. Sage sat on the edge of the king-size bed while her mother freshened her lipstick in the bathroom and her Dad arranged his favorite two Stetsons on the top rack of the narrow closet. Sage was getting claustrophobic and wanted to head out already. Her parents had arrived in Tenacity just twenty minutes ago, checked in, and called Sage to come over so they could go to the Silver Spur for breakfast—like old times.

The phrase *old times* had made her wince. From here on in, everything had to be about *new* times. The town. Sage's life and career. Her deep connection with Brent Woodson.

"Another plus of a dinosaur park bringing in revenue and visitors to Tenacity is that nicer hotels and inns will be built," Rosemary Abernathy said as she emerged from the bathroom, tucking a strand of her bobbed ash-blond hair behind one ear. Sage had gotten her blond hair from both parents, but she had her dad's brown eyes. Her mother's were a beautiful blue, but right now Rosemary's gaze was narrowed on the wall art around the room. She frowned and shook her head. "The room is clean but just so *basic*. Sometimes it's nice to be pampered."

"Pampered in Tenacity?" Bert Abernathy snorted. "This town hasn't changed in the fifteen years since we left."

"Well, as Mom just noted, that *is* about to change," Sage said. "And I wouldn't be surprised if a luxury hotel goes up within three months of the park opening and being a smash success. A dinosaur park is unique, educational, fun, and for people of *all* ages. It'll absolutely drive tourism—and the need for all kinds of accommodations, restaurants, and businesses."

"It does sound exciting," her mom said, grabbing her coat. "When I first read about the foundation for revitalizing Tenacity, I thought, oh please—déjà vu from fifteen years ago. Never happened. But there's a real energy around this new push. And with bones found recently? Right here in Tenacity? I think investing in this venture is a great idea."

"Agreed," Bert said, standing up. He chose his black Stetson and put on his wool coat.

Sage's heart gave a little leap. Now, this was the kind of conversation she was happy to partake in.

They headed out to the elevator and ran into the Farmingtons, a couple around the same age as her parents. Sage remembered them from when she was growing up. They'd been considered well-to-do and on the snooty side. They all greeted one another, catching up as they waited for the elevator doors to open.

"We're also just visiting," Ella Farmington said. "We moved about ten years ago when it was clear Tenacity was going downhill. Businesses closing up. All because of what happened with that stolen money." She mock-shivered. "You two were right to leave when you did."

"Well, we're moving back," Rosemary said, her chin up in what Sage knew was her defensive posture. "Didn't you hear about the plans for the dinosaur park? Tenacity is going to be a major destination in a couple of years. We're early adopters—planning to not only invest in the park but to buy a ranch in town before land values skyrocket."

"I don't know," Douglas Farmington said. "To tell you the truth, I don't like that the foundation is being run by *those two*. There's just something sordid about the whole thing."

Sage's heart sank and she glanced at her parents, who looked confused.

"Those two?" Rosemary repeated, tilting her head quizzically. "I know Seth Taylor is part of the revitalization efforts. He's a great guy. His family and the Abernathys are connected through marriage. Who's the other guy?"

"I'm talking about Barrett Deroy and Brent Woodson," Douglas said. "Is Seth Taylor related to the Taylor Beef empire?" His eyes lit up at the prospect. "That's a big deal if he's part of things too."

Bert nodded. "He is. Now, wait a second—Barrett Deroy? Isn't he the one who stole the money in the first place? We left soon after that happened and didn't keep up with town news."

Sage deflated even more as Ella Farmington launched into the story she said she'd just heard in town last night. Adultery, theft, blackmail. "Can you believe all that went on in tiny Tenacity? My goodness."

"The Woodsons?" Rosemary repeated, blinking. "I never would have imagined that from June and Clifford."

Ella shook her head. "And that's not all. People are saying their son, Brent, knew all about it. All the single women in Tenacity considered him *the* catch until the truth broke. Now he apparently can't get a date to save his life."

A burst of red-hot anger ignited in Sage. Was steam blowing out of her ears? She was about to launch into her own little monologue and defend Brent, but she was suddenly aware of her mother staring at her, Rosemary looking kind of pale. She had no doubt what her mom was thinking: *Brent Woodson—that cocky jock we found out you were secretly dating fifteen years ago? Since you've been in town for a few days, you clearly must have heard all about this scandal and you didn't tell us? You think we'll hand over money to a swindler? He'll probably turn around and invest it in some Ponzi scheme! Wait till we tell Seth who's he's gotten mixed up with!*

Yes, Sage could see all that in her mother's stony expression.

She took a breath. "I happen to know Brent Woodson," she said to the Farmingtons. "He had no idea about either of his parents' actions fifteen years ago. He found out the truth when everyone else did—six months ago. He's an honest, honorable, good person who's having to deal with a lot of unfair speculation and gossip. The town means everything to him. And the foundation—and what the dinosaur park could mean for Tenacity—is his way to help set things right." There was no need to add that she knew all this because she'd gotten *very* close to Brent while she'd been back in town; that was better suited to a private conversation with her parents. Not the gossip-hungry Farmingtons.

"Who knows *what* to think?" Ella said, her husband nodding beside her.

The steam continued to build. Sage was truly surprised no one could see it pouring from her ears.

Her mother seemed about to blurt out something but clearly thought better of it because she clamped her mouth shut. "Well, isn't that all very interesting," Rosemary finally said, eyes narrowing farther as she slid a glance at Sage. "We had *no* idea about *any* of this."

Sage swallowed. Breakfast at the Silver Spur was going to be something.

The elevator came just then, and as they all rode down, she could feel her mother's gaze boring into her as Sage stared straight ahead at the row of numbers on the panel. Mrs. Farmington kept up a steady stream of chitchat about how she'd recently dined at Castillo's and it was even better than she remembered and the Abernathys simply had to go and try the steak fajitas.

"Sizzling," Ella added as the doors pinged open. "Bye now," she said, and the Farmingtons headed out.

"Well, this changes a few things," Rosemary said with a frown as they walked toward the door. "I don't think we can invest in good conscience."

Sage stopped and stared at her mother. "Why? Doesn't what I said in Brent's defense mean anything?"

"Sweetheart," Rosemary said, resuming walking, "you're letting nostalgia and sweet memories for an old flame affect how you're thinking."

That was definitely not the case. "I've gotten to know Brent Woodson while I've been back," Sage said as they exited the hotel. "I believe he knew nothing about what his parents did. He's changed so much the past six months. And Tenacity is extremely important to him. The foundation, the dinosaur park—he's putting his heart and soul into it."

"Well, he's certainly sold you," her mother said.

Grrr, her mother was so frustrating! *Keep calm and make your case*, she told herself.

"Let's talk about it over breakfast," Sage said. "I believe in Brent and in the foundation and what the dinosaur park will mean to Tenacity—to those land values you were talking about too. And I'd like you to hear me out."

"Of course we'll listen, honey," her father said. "But does the apple fall far from the tree?"

Sage sucked in a breath. "Yes, it often does. I knew plenty of mean kids who had the loveliest parents. I knew plenty of mean adults who had the sweetest kids."

"I suppose," Rosemary said as they walked toward the Silver Spur. "But I'm no longer feeling good about handing over a big chunk of money. Seth called me while we were driving here and talked up the foundation. We arranged a meeting tomorrow to talk about us investing, but maybe we'll cancel. He'll just have to understand."

Sage sighed. She'd been determined to use her voice with her parents, and she was off to a great start. Over omelets and pancakes and coffee, she'd lay out the reasons why they should invest in the park. She'd never stood up for herself before, but she'd stand up for Tenacity. And for Brent.

Brent had just slipped his mare an apple slice in the far pasture after examining the fence line when Sage called. It was just past noon. He knew she'd met her parents for breakfast, so this call could be good news or very bad news.

"Hey," he said. "How are you?" No matter what, he also knew Sage was going through a lot where the Abernathys were concerned.

"I'll be honest. I'm tense. I made the case for why I think my parents should invest in the park, but they're focused on events that have nothing to do with the foundation."

His heart sank. "Like my family. They're worried that I'm not ethical?"

She was quiet for a moment. "Yeah. I'm sorry, Brent. They would like to get together, though. The four of us. To hear from you face-to-face. What do you think?"

He instantly brightened. "I think that's great. That means they're giving me a chance. And I think they'll be able to hear the conviction in my voice, see the honesty in my face."

"I could not agree more," she said.

"Was the meeting their idea or yours?" he asked.

"Okay, mine. But they're willing to hear you out. And that's the key. I heard you speak at the inauguration, Brent. Your commitment to Tenacity, your passion for the project—once they spend two minutes in your company, they'll believe in you too."

He felt a burst of warmth ward off the chill in his chest. *Her* belief in him meant the world to him. "I appreciate that. I hope you know that. I appreciate *you*. And I'm grateful for this opportunity to talk to them, Sage. I don't know if you've told them we're seeing each other, and you certainly don't have to at this point. But I do like the idea of being able to win them over on that angle too." His chest was tightening as he spoke, though. What if he *couldn't* win them over? On either point?

"Well, just remember that I'm my own woman, Brent. If they're more drawn by negative gossip from strangers than the assurance of their own daughter, then that'll tell me a few things. But for you, just remember that they're hard nuts to crack. It's not necessarily *you* or me, really, it's *them*. That might sound like the oldest line in the book, but when it comes to them, it fits."

He could barely eke a smile. "But I care about you, Sage. And they're your parents. So what they think matters to me."

"They'll see who you are. I really believe that."

An idea came to him. A good one, he was pretty sure. "What do you think about having them over to my house? I'll cook. They'll see me at my ranch, in my home, and be able to get to know me a little better that way. It'll be less formal than dinner out somewhere."

"That's a great idea," she said, her voice brightening. "Absolutely perfect. Six thirty?"

"I'll see you all then. And, Sage, thank you. Even if they hate my guts and tell me they won't invest in the park and that the idea of us as a couple makes them sick, I'll just be glad to see your beautiful face again for a couple of hours."

"Aw thank you. But think positively, okay?"

"I'll try," he said.

Even as they disconnected, he wished she were still on the other end.

For this very important dinner, Brent had decided on steak—Taylor Beef, of course—roast potatoes, and asparagus. A meal fit for ranchers. That was one thing he and the Abernathys had in common and hopefully would go a long way in finding common ground and building good will.

He'd tidied up the house, which looked warm and welcoming. The dining room table, which he rarely ever used, was set, the kitchen smelled amazing, and he was—

The doorbell rang.

Brent sucked in a breath. *You've got this*, he told himself.

The Abernathy family stood on his doorstep, Sage holding a large bag from the bakery.

"Come on in out of the cold," Brent said, stepping aside so they could enter.

The Abernathys hung up their coats on the wrought-iron rack by the door, the elder two staring at him. They weren't looking around or making small talk. Just staring.

He cleared his throat. "I'm very happy to meet you both. And that you're giving me the opportunity to discuss how important the dinosaur park is to Tenacity."

He waited a beat to see if the Abernathys would say anything, but they remained silent, both giving slight nods. They were mid to late fifties and looked alike with the same coloring as Sage. They hadn't exactly met all those years ago, but they'd seen one another around town back then.

"Mom, Dad, you remember Brent Woodson," Sage said with a warm smile. "Brent, my parents, Rosemary and Bert Abernathy."

"Nice to see you again," Brent said.

Bert smiled, which helped build Brent's confidence a bit. It deflated some when Rosemary raked her assessing gaze over him.

Bert walked over to the wide living room windows that showed a section of pasture and the beautiful red barn. "Nice operation," he said. "I can see it's well taken care of."

Rosemary joined her husband and nodded. "We're planning on buying a ranch not too far from here. About ten minutes. Good land, nice house and outbuildings. We'll bring up our animals, and given the size of the property, we'll be able to add to our herd."

Brent realized that they wouldn't go through with buying property if they didn't feel confident that the dinosaur park would actually come into fruition, even if they didn't trust him or even Barrett to invest. That actually gave him a little more confidence at reaching them.

For a few minutes they talked about ranch life; then Brent said he'd better check on the steaks and asked what they'd like to drink, that he had just about everything. Bert and Rosemary opted for water, and Sage offered to come help.

In the kitchen, Sage stepped close to him. "It's going well!" she whispered.

"So far, so good." He could tell the Abernathys were tightly wound, but they'd been here all of five minutes. Once they sat down at the table and felt a bit more comfortable, they'd all loosen up.

Sage brought their drinks to them while Brent plated the steaks and asparagus, then added the potatoes. Everything looked great—if he did say so himself. Sage returned and they each carried out a tray containing two plates. Brent served, and they all sat down at the table.

Mrs. Abernathy complimented the food, and Mr. Abernathy declared the steaks excellent.

"Taylor Beef," Brent said since it was also a good segue. "Seth Taylor has become a good friend, and he let me know he spoke to you about possibly investing in the dinosaur park. If you have any additional questions or concerns," he added with some emphasis, "I'm happy to discuss anything honestly and openly."

"That's good to hear," Rosemary said. "I say we enjoy this lovely dinner, then talk business. How long have you owned this ranch?"

Brent relaxed immediately. He *could* enjoy his food now. They'd save the harder conversation for coffee and dessert. "Close to five years. I studied ranch management in college—locally—and then worked at some large ranches in the area. I presented the bank with a solid business plan for a loan and bought Big Sky when it was failing and turned the ranch around. It's hard work every day, but I love it."

"Very impressive," Bert said, and Brent could see he meant it.

"Agreed," Rosemary added. "It couldn't have been easy getting a ranch up and running in Tenacity without working very hard and long hours, putting back every cent into the place."

Okay, this *was* going well. He glanced at Sage, and she looked very pleased.

He talked about making some smart investments of his own that had paid off, allowing him to pay off the original loan and add to the land and the herd.

"Speaking of investments," Rosemary said, putting her fork down. They'd all made quick work of their meals, and the time had come to get down to why they were here. "We did talk to Seth on the phone, and plan to see him tomorrow. We're *thinking* about investing in the dinosaur park, but—"

But…

"We're not going to mince words," Bert finished. "We did hear about the terrible story that came out six months ago concerning your family and the Deroys." He shook his head. "We made a few calls to people we used to know in town and asked their thoughts. About *you*. About whether or not we can put our trust in you. Our investment in the park wouldn't be chump change."

Brent swallowed. Some people thought he was complicit. Some people thought he was as innocent in all this as Barrett had been.

"I personally vouched for Brent this morning," Sage said, looking very uncomfortable. And a bit angry. "I expect that to mean more than what some old acquaintances from fifteen years ago speculate."

"Honey, of course your opinion means more," Rosemary said. "But you were sweet on Brent fifteen years ago, and I have the feeling you are now too. I could see that all over your face earlier when you were defending him. So that colors things."

Talk about coloring things. Sage's cheeks were turning pink.

"To be open and honest, I am 'sweet on him.' I believe in Brent. I believed in him fifteen years ago because I saw underneath the golden-boy aura. And I believe in him now. I've heard him talk about the past and the future with such heart, such conviction. This is a man who cares deeply about Tenacity. About righting wrongs—not his own, but his parents'. He's paying for being a Woodson, and that's not fair."

The Abernathys were both staring at Sage, looking as uncomfortable as she had a minute ago. They'd clearly come here with their minds made up, and that their daughter was fighting for him so vehemently was throwing a wrench in things.

Brent turned to Sage. "That means so much to me, Sage. Thank you." He looked at Rosemary and Bert Abernathy. "I understand your concern. I know there are still many in town who think I must have been in on it. But I assure you I wasn't. I care a lot about getting my good name back. Rebuilding it, I should say. But I care more about this town. Its future. I'm not my parents, Mr. and Mrs. Abernathy. I'm my own man and always have been. And these past six months, I've grown into someone who I actually like. That took a while."

Rosemary lifted her chin. "And you and Sage are dating?"

Brent would let their daughter answer that. The way she wanted to.

"We are," Sage said. "I haven't been this happy in a long time."

Both parents were staring at her, something shifting in their expressions, but whether they were moved by anything either of them said, he had no idea. They *were* hard nuts.

"How do we know all this—your work on the foundation, for the dinosaur park—isn't just about optics?" Bert asked. "To get that good name back—if you even had it to begin with," he added on something of a cough.

Brent forced the frown off his face. He launched into how much the park meant to him, how much Tenacity meant. That he was here for good, that he wouldn't run away to start over, that he'd rebuild himself right here where he was born and raised—and ruined. He'd fight for himself and the town.

"Personally, I could clap," Sage said to her parents. "I wish you saw and heard what *I* do."

"Well, sweetheart, you're a little biased," her mother said. "You *are* dating him."

"As for…the past, the truth always does come out eventually, doesn't it," Bert said in a statement. "So I guess we'll see."

They were not on board. That was clear. Not about him being part of the foundation. Not about him dating their daughter. She hardly needed their approval on that part anymore, but he knew their blessing meant something to her—that it would make her happy.

"Let me ask you this, Brent," her dad added. "Are you going to sit here and tell us that working on the foundation and giving speeches about the dinosaur park hasn't helped your reputation?"

Brent winced at the element of truth to her father's words. When he'd first decided to work with Barrett back in the summer, he had hoped their joint venture would improve his image in Tenacity. Back then, he was first and foremost a politician's son.

But that had changed fast. When the shock had started wearing off. When reality had hit him square in the face. He didn't like who he'd been. He'd pretty much been the last to know his own mother was having an affair. Apparently, that had been town gossip, but Brent had never heard about it. Maybe because he'd been too popular, too arrogant, too much of a bully for anyone to dare talk about that kind of thing around him. Instead, they'd whispered behind his back.

For months now, he'd been working on being a better person. He now believed he was someone who deserved Sage Abernathy in his life. He wanted to tell her parents that, how meaningful that was, but he knew they weren't ready to hear it. They didn't think he deserved her. And they didn't think any foundation that trusted him deserved their hard-earned money. He could see it on their faces. His character was in question.

"I'm going to be very honest, Mr. and Mrs. Abernathy. If my parents' actions hadn't come to light, if I'd never found out about what they'd both done, I would likely have tossed some money at new revitalization efforts and not thought about it beyond that. That's who I used to be—someone who was self-absorbed. More interested in myself than others."

He glanced at Sage, who was looking at him with such encouragement, such trust, that it spurred him to go on.

"But when my entire life was turned upside down," he continued, "I had to really look at who I was, where I'd come from, who I wanted to be. Do I care what people think? Yes, I do. Did accepting Barrett's offer to work with him on the foundation help turn public opinion about me for the better? Yes, to a degree. But I'm putting so much of myself into the revitalization efforts because of how much I care about this town. And because it's my own way of trying to right some wrongs that involved my family." He inwardly let out the breath he'd been holding. He'd meant every word of that.

The Abernathys seemed to take that in, but their expressions didn't change a whit.

"Brent, we thank you for dinner," Rosemary said. "It was absolutely delicious. Nothing like Taylor Beef."

Nothing like all he just said being completely ignored. He'd tried and that was all he could do.

"It was my pleasure," he said. "And I appreciate that you gave me the chance to speak directly to you. That means a lot to me."

"Well, we have a lot to consider," Bert said. With that, both Abernathy parents rose.

"I'm going to stay awhile," Sage said to her folks. "Brent will drop me at the hotel later."

Rosemary lifted her chin. "You're coming to see the ranch with us in the morning, right? Bright and early at eight o'clock."

"I'll meet you in the lobby, then," she said.

Brent wondered if Sage still wanted to. She probably hoped that after a night's sleep, they'd see things differently. And maybe a new conversation would start.

They all walked to the front door. The Abernathys put on their coats, Bert put on his Stetson, they hugged Sage goodbye, Bert shook Brent's hand, and then they were gone. Brent and Sage stayed on the porch and watched their taillights disappear down the long drive.

Sage wrapped her arms around him. "I love what you said, Brent. I felt all that come straight from your heart. My parents will come around. About you, about investing, *and* about us."

What would he do without her faith in him—in *them*? He held on to her tightly, but the cold air got to be too much.

"Let's go sit by the fire," he said.

She smiled and nodded. "Everything is going to be all right," she said. "I know it."

He hugged her and they went back in. But as they sat on the rug in front of the fireplace, barely having the coffee and cake that her parents hadn't stuck around for, he realized he'd been missing something. An important step.

Maybe the Abernathys, like others in town, couldn't get a good read on him because his past wasn't quite resolved. And if he was going to come to terms with that past, get comfortable in his present, and look forward to his future, he had to *deal* with it. Which meant going to see his father.

Brent had sat down with his mother a few times the past six months, had some heart-to-hearts, and he'd believed her when she sobbed that she was so sorry, that if she could take it all back, she would. Falling for her first love when she'd been married with two kids. Planning to run away with him. Stealing the money to finance her divorce and the bitter custody hearing she'd figuring was coming. She'd felt desperate and she'd done terrible things. All these years, she'd known Barrett Deroy hadn't stolen Tenacity's future from it, but she'd said nothing. And just let the money stay where it was, even if she kept saying that Clifford must have hidden it. Maybe. But Brent had been able to read his father pretty well these days, and he'd insisted he hadn't touched the cash.

In any case, Brent would get so frustrated at the unanswered questions that he'd leave in frustration. Add to that Brent demanding the truth from his dad about the election interference back in November and getting nowhere, and Brent had avoided dealing with Cliff since. At home alone, he'd think: Part of her penance was having to stay married to Cliff Woodson for another fifteen years. Brent could see that she was trying to do whatever she could to earn his and his sister's respect again. Including staying in town, despite how far she'd fallen from grace. Whereas June Woodson had stayed in Tenacity to face up to her past, to seek forgiveness from the people and town she'd wronged, Clifford Woodson had stayed because he didn't think he'd done anything wrong.

Talking to his dad had been maddening. Clifford was unapologetic. Smug. Everything was someone else's fault. *My wife was cheating on me! About to leave me for that lowlife farrier! I was so mad and hurt, I lashed out, trying to hurt them both as badly as I was. I never said Barrett Jr. stole the money, just that I'd start the rumor he had unless the Deroys left town. People came to their own conclusions when they fled!* Then Cliff would start sobbing—sorry *not* for how he'd ruined a teenage boy's reputation, but for *himself.* He'd lost his job as mayor, his standing in town, and most people's respect.

Brent needed to wrap his head around who his father was. If he could do that, if he could just find a

way to deal with his father going from his hero to...
Brent didn't know what. Just someone he didn't want
to be like. Ever.

If he wanted to become a person he could be proud
of—and someday be a good husband and father—he'd
need to resolve this knot in his chest, the bitterness in
his gut. It was time to have a real talk with Cliff Woodson. Maybe then he'd be in a better place, in a better
position to show people—like the Abernathys—who
he was.

He looked over at the beautiful woman at his side,
this extraordinary woman who believed in him. For
their future, he'd go see his dad and not leave until
he'd found some measure of peace.

Chapter Nine

Last night wasn't exactly like the previous evening she'd spent with Brent, waking in his arms without a care, their focus only on each other. After her parents had left, it had taken her a while to come down from how upset she'd been. How awful they'd been about Brent, *to* Brent. How they'd dismissed her take on the situation because she had feelings for him. So she and Brent had spent the night together, but they'd each been preoccupied. Things were so heavy so soon into their new relationship. She'd gotten a firsthand glimpse into what his life had been like the past six months, the judgment from the town and from her own parents. And she'd been furious—and unable to shake it.

Brent had been preoccupied, too, and they'd both given each other space to sit with their gloomy thoughts while finding solace in being together. She'd given him a silent back massage; he'd given her a silent foot massage. Every now and then, he'd squeeze her hand or she'd press a hand to his shoulder, his knee. An acknowledgment that they were there for each other but lost in their own thoughts.

They hadn't made love. But they had spooned together, Brent kissing her cheek or shoulder several times, tracing a finger down her cheek, running a hand down her hair. In the middle of the night, she felt him tightening his hold on her as if he was afraid of losing her, and her heart swelled for him.

This morning, Brent had made her breakfast, and they'd been quiet again. She'd wanted to tell him everything would be okay, but honestly, she didn't know. Her parents had to be weighing heavily on him.

And when he'd walked her to the door, he told her that he'd understand if the fact that her parents couldn't give their blessing for their relationship made her want to take a step back.

She'd felt tears sting her eyes.

Absolutely not, she'd told him. *What matters to me is how we feel about each other. No one else.*

He'd hugged her goodbye with such tenderness, such emotion. And it had been very hard to rip herself away to go meet her parents in the lobby at the hotel.

If she'd expected an apology or for them to say they would be giving deep consideration to all Brent had said, to all she had said, it hadn't come. Rosemary and Bert had said they didn't want to discuss anything about last night while they were focused on making a major real estate purchase. They put in an offer on the place at 8:30 a.m. By nine, the house was theirs. And though the closing wouldn't be for another month, the owners, who'd already downsized to a small house in town, told the Abernathys they could come and go as they pleased to plan and measure.

Sage had taken that to heart. She wanted to spend

some time at the property, walk the land, breathe the air, see how she felt. She didn't want to make a decision about her future, where she'd live, what she'd do out of frustration at her parents. She wanted to make the choice strictly for *herself.*

The ranch was beautiful, thirty-five hundred acres with a long tree-lined drive, a lovely two-story white house with a red door and wraparound porch, well-tended outbuildings, and fencing around several pastures. She could see why her parents had chosen it. But as she'd toured the house and land with them earlier, she'd felt...nothing. Granted, nothing about the place was familiar. It wasn't home.

But *would* it be home? If she moved here with her parents, she'd slowly warm up to the ranch like she had in Cheyenne all those years ago. She'd find things she loved about it, from the way the sun set over the mountains to finding certain trees to set up an easel under. But this move was different; she wasn't a fifteen-year-old with no choice. Yes, she could have moved out on her own over the years, but this time, she was being handed a perfect opportunity to make the break she'd been thinking about for a while.

So now, just after 10:00 a.m., Sage had driven back out to the ranch without her parents, who had gone back to the hotel to start making arrangements to put their Cheyenne property up for sale. Sketch pad on her lap and her box of pastels beside her, she sat on the porch steps of the house bundled up in her jacket and scarf and hat, grateful it wasn't too cold and appreciating the charm of the place. This ranch was almost twice the size of the one they were selling in Cheyenne. Her parents would make a mint from the sale and would be able to add to their herd, buy new equipment and hire new staff.

Sage stared up at her subject—the black wrought-iron weathervane atop the beautiful gray barn about one hundred feet away. The ranch was completely empty and quiet, the sky slightly overcast, and Sage was itching to capture the moodiness in her sketch. Sometimes she drew first, then painted from her drawing, liking how her imagination came into play.

She started with a dark gray pencil, but something felt off, and she shifted over a few inches but that didn't help. She kept at it and she'd captured the top of barn and the weathervane just fine, but there was nothing special about it. It was just a drawing. She could work at it, fine-tuning the shadowing, but she instinctively knew that the problem was inside her. Sage could feel inspiration anywhere, in the most ordinary of places, but everything in her seemed to be saying it was time to go, find her own place, forge her own path.

Just the thought sent a tingle in her hand, almost making the pencil vibrate. Yup, there it was. The inspiration.

She closed her eyes and smiled, the surety of her decision filling her with equal parts peace and excitement. She was doing this. Striking out on her own, going her own way. Sage had saved up quite a bit of money over the years. If she was financially careful— and she would be—she'd only have to supplement her income with a part-time job. She had a small trust fund she'd gotten on her twenty-first birthday, but she'd never touched it, and wouldn't except in a dire emergency. She always saw that money as being for the family she'd have one day, security, a down-payment on a house, college for her kids if they chose to go.

I want to stay in Tenacity. That, she knew for sure. This hardscrabble town that had been through so much had once been home and still felt like it. Her parents would be here—even if they made her insane. She was rekindling old friendships. And she had a boyfriend here, she thought with a smile, warmth flooding her.

Maybe she'd take a big chunk of her savings and buy a very small ranch of her own, nonworking, but she'd have a horse and a two-bedroom cabin, one for herself, one for a painting studio. Or maybe she'd find an apartment around Central Avenue and be more in town. She could do anything she wanted.

Including have her boyfriend sleep over. Brent's handsome face floated into her mind. She couldn't wait to see him again, to tell him about her plans.

Her parents might not believe in him, but she did. And for this new Sage Abernathy, that was what mattered.

Sage flipped a page in her sketchbook and started the drawing anew. This time, the weathervane came to life against the bleak sky and the icy gray of the barn's steeply pitched roof. Her heart leaped. She flipped back to the previous page and signed it at the bottom with *Before*. Then she turned ahead to the new drawing and signed it *After*.

She heard a car approaching and glanced over at

the drive. Her parents' SUV was making its way toward the house.

Sage sucked in a breath. Well, as the saying went, there was no time like the present. She'd tell them about her plan. Would they be upset? Would they be happy for her? She wasn't quite sure. If her dad didn't want to take on the job of handling the ranch finances, they could easily hire someone trustworthy from word of mouth. She wasn't leaving them in the lurch. Maybe they'd even say: *Sage, we're so proud of you. You're thirty and it's a milestone time of self-reflection. You're making a positive change, and good for you.*

Maybe.

Her parents had beaming smiles as they got out of the car, looking all around with such excitement, her mother's hand on her heart. Her father held a big metal tape measure.

"Sage, what a surprise to see you here," her mom said as they approached the porch. "Picking out your bedroom?"

Sage inwardly flinched. *There is your in, girl. Go for it.*

She stood—and stood proud. "Actually, Mom, Dad, I've come to a decision. I'm going to move to Tenacity—but to my own place. I've long wanted to focus on my art, and that's what I'm going to do. I have a couple of ideas for who might take over the handling of the ranch finances—"

"Honey," her mother interrupted with a scowl, "just because we don't see eye to eye on a couple of issues doesn't mean—"

"My decision has nothing to do with last night," Sage interrupted. "It has to do with me. With living my own life, pursuing my own dreams, going my own way. I'm thirty—it's high time for me to have my own place."

Sage looked at her parents. Her dad seemed surprised but had a thoughtful expression on his face, which she appreciated. Her mother had a half scowl on her face. Sage also saw something else—disappointment. Not in Sage, exactly. But in the fact that she'd no longer be living with them. She knew her mother very well, and that flicker of emotion helped soften her ire at Rosemary Abernathy.

"But, Sage, art is a *hobby*," her mother said. "Something people do in their spare time and on weekends."

Sage inwardly sighed. A lot of people saw it that way. "I'd like to pursue it more seriously. I've sold a few of my watercolor sketches and paintings through my online shop, and—"

"Well, I don't think it's a good idea, Sage," Rosemary said. "We had such a nice family operation going in Cheyenne, and now we'll continue that here. It's best for everyone—especially you. There's no security in painting, honey. Tell her, Bert."

Sage's father tilted his head. "Well, I don't know, Rosemary," he said, looking at Sage with that same thoughtful expression. "If Sage wants to go in a new direction, that's up to her."

There it was. She had a feeling her father would be able to talk her mother down about all this. It might take a while for Rosemary to come around. But that was fine with Sage.

She would have grabbed her dad into a big bear hug, but she didn't want to rub anything in her mother's face—and her dad would certainly get the silent treatment later until her mother would start to come around in a few days. A few *months*, maybe.

Rosemary Abernathy lifted her chin. "I'd like you to think more about this, Sage. Your place is at the family business. We need you at the ranch."

"Mom, I have thought about this long and hard. This is eight years in the making. Longer, since I originally wanted to study art in college and felt obligated to follow the path you wanted instead. I'm going to live on my own and focus on painting. It's time, Mom. I really hope you can understand."

"Well, I don't understand," Rosemary said, throwing up her hands. "Bert, you have nothing to say?"

"Rosemary," her father said, "it's Sage's decision. It's *her* life. And to be honest, I can easily take over handling the books."

I knew it—thank you, Dad!

Her mother was slowly shaking her head, giving her husband the stink-eye. She turned to Sage with a full scowl now. "Well, we have something to share with *you*. Dad and I decided we're not investing in the dinosaur park."

Sage gasped, her heart plummeting. "Because I'm moving out on my own?"

"No, it has nothing to do with that," her mom said. "Ask your father, we decided this last night."

Her father nodded. "We did. We talked about it and just don't feel comfortable putting our hard-earned money into something we can't fully trust in. Maybe if it was just Seth and Barrett Deroy on the foundation. But a Woodson? Honey, the lack of ethics in that family…"

Rosemary mock-shivered.

A hot burst of anger flamed in Sage's gut. "I'm surprised you'd even trust me to continue handling the ranch's finances, if you don't trust my judgment when it comes to men. You know that I'm dating Brent Woodson."

"Sage, we're sorry," her dad said, looking somewhat contrite but steadfast nonetheless. "You're on cloud nine in a new romance, and that's clouded your thinking."

And she'd thought her father was on her side?

"You're my parents and I love you," she said, disappointment punching her repeatedly in the stomach. "But I think you're being unfair and extremely judgmental. Brent told you, from his heart and very eloquently, why you should feel comfortable and safe trusting him. And I vouched for him. That means so little?"

Rosemary practically rolled her eyes. "Like Dad said, you're clouded by your new romance. You're not seeing things clearly."

"I absolutely am," Sage said. "All I can say is that I hope you give him more consideration and change your mind. I believe in Brent. So does the person most wronged by his parents—Barrett Deroy. And so does

Seth Taylor. That should be enough for you. But you're letting gossip from people you don't even know anymore dictate what you do."

"The subject is closed," Rosemary said.

Sage mentally shook her head, so frustrated she could let out a big scream. "I need to get going. I *am* sorry we don't see eye to eye. On any subject. I'll see you later."

Her mother seemed about to say something but remained quiet. Her father sent her an apologetic look, but he was clearly as down on Brent as her mother was.

Brent—the man Sage was falling hard for.

Tears stung her eyes, and that hot burst of anger flamed brighter as she headed to her car. She'd expected to celebrate her big decision, her new life plan. But all she felt like doing was crying.

Brent had finished his midmorning chores at the ranch and forced himself into his pickup at noon. What he really wanted to do was go see Sage, just hold her, make sure she was holding up after that disaster of a dinner last night, but he knew that if he was going to give his all to their relationship, he needed to pull a Barrett Deroy and *deal* with things.

So Brent would go to the family home and sit down with his dad over lunch in the kitchen. Casual, just the two of them, over sandwiches. Maybe he'd get some answers. Find some peace. Settle something that had long been festering inside him. He hadn't spoken to his father since November, when everyone found out about the fixed election.

Brent knew his dad had had a hand in that. There was no evidence, not like the texts between Moore and Garrett about tampered-with ballots, but based on a few things his father had said, how smug he'd been right before the election, little things. Brent *knew*. He'd gone from completely clueless to extremely aware.

He likely wouldn't run into his mother, who, according to his sister, spent a lot of time in her bedroom, knitting hats and sweaters for local charities. He supposed they all had their own ways of dealing with the fallout, and right now, keeping a very low profile while trying to do some good was June's.

He pulled into the driveway. No cars, but there was a garage, and both his parents' vehicles were likely inside. He walked up to the front door and sucked in a breath and stared up at the sky for a moment, the overcast day suiting his mood. He rang the bell. And waited. Silence.

He grabbed his phone and called his sister. "I'm at the house, but no one's answering. Any idea where Dad is hanging out these days?"

"Actually, yes," she said. "Apparently, Mom and Dad got into a huge argument and she demanded he move out and that they put the house on the market immediately so they could be done with each other. And he said fine, he was done with her anyway. So Mom screamed back, 'I was done with you first!' He's been staying at the Tenacity Inn and booked a room at the *monthly* rate. I was planning on calling you tonight with the latest, but honestly, I'm trying not to think about them too much."

Brent sighed. "I hear you. You okay?"

"I guess. It's a long time coming. They stayed together for fifteen years while holding on to information about each other that had to make them both sick."

"Right? Dad knew Mom was having an affair and was about to leave him, that she'd stolen the money. And Mom knew Dad had blackmailed her boyfriend to leave town with his family. *Fifteen years* they both lived with that—and the two of us knew nothing about it. My God, Vick, when I put it that way, I can see why most folks in town think I was in on it."

Victoria was quiet for a second; then he heard a little sniffle, as if she'd held her phone away from her ear so he wouldn't realize she was crying.

"Hey, it's okay, Victoria. We're dealing with things. We've both made major changes in our lives, right? You moved out immediately. You have your job at the consignment shop, which you really like. And you'll always have me."

She seemed to be sniffling harder. "I love you, Brent. I don't know what I'd do if I didn't have you."

"You'll never have to know. How about I take you out to lunch instead of going to see Dad. I'm sure I won't get the answers I'm looking for anyway. And he'll be in a foul mood."

"I'm meeting Cassie for lunch in a little while, but thanks anyway." She waited a beat, then said, "What answers are you looking for? I mean, do you think there's more you could hear that would help you make peace with everything?"

"I think I just want Dad to say, 'Yes, Brent, I did terrible things, and then I said I'd change and I didn't, and I'm sorry. You and your sister are everything to me and being a better person for you two is all that matters.'"

"Brent..." Victoria said. He could almost see her shaking her head at how naive her big brother was.

"I know," he said. "But I need *something*. Something to help me at least put that part of the past behind me so I can focus on being that better person. For you. And for Sage."

He heard an intake of breath. "Sage? You two are dating?"

"It's new, but yes. And I really care about her. I want this to work. And for me to really let go, to really be fully there for the relationship, I need to deal with my past."

She was quiet again for a moment. "I get it. Oh, I have to go. A few people just came into the shop. Good luck if you see Dad."

"Thanks. You call me if you ever need anything or just to talk, okay?"

She promised she would, and they disconnected, Brent feeling better just from the conversation with Victoria. Thank God he had her. She was the one bright spot in his family, in the mess the two of them were left to clean up. He hoped she'd come out of the shell she'd built around herself these past six months and let love into her life. Brent would always be there for her, but his sister could definitely use that special someone in her life. Maybe in the coming months, she'd start dating again. Victoria had always been private, ever since she'd hit tweenhood, but ever since the truth had come out about their parents, she'd kept a very low profile.

Feeling better from talking to his sister, he went back to his pickup. Time to head to the Tenacity Inn—and unfortunately *not* to see Sage.

Chapter Ten

Just as Brent was walking toward the front doors of the Tenacity Inn, a very familiar tall figure, University of Montana baseball cap pulled low on his head, was coming out of the Silver Spur Café with a take-out bag and heading for the hotel, eyes downcast.

Clifford Woodson—looking rough.

His father wore a navy down jacket and gray sweatpants and sneakers. He looked tired, haggard—and miserable.

Brent braced himself, then called out, "Dad."

His father's hopeful expression as he looked up at the voice of his son poked at Brent's heart. Brent stopped in front of the hotel, his father jogging over. "Are you a sight for sore eyes!" Clifford said with a smile, life coming back into his face. "Does this mean you're speaking to me again?"

Again, dagger to the chest. He loved his father, always would. But he did not like the man he now knew his father to be. "I'm hoping we can talk—that you'll help me find some peace about everything that's happened."

Cliff's eyes lit up. "I can do that." He held up the

take-out bag. I got a burger and fries. "We can split it or we can go get another."

"I ate at home," Brent said, pushing open the door to the hotel.

"Speaking of *home*, this is mine now," Cliff said in his most forlorn voice, matching his expression. Within a minute, the old Clifford Woodson was back, the one desperate to curry sympathy and support. "Your mother told me to leave—for the hundredth time—and she made me mad enough that I did."

Brent was not interested in talking about his parents' marriage. That was between Clifford and June. He stopped and turned to his dad and looked him square in the eye. "I want you to promise me something, Dad. That you will not drag Victoria into your problems with Mom or try to get her to take sides. Vick deserves better than that."

Clifford frowned. "Of course. I'd never!"

Sure you would, Dad, Brent thought, but he was letting it go. He'd gotten the promise, and that would have to stand right now.

As they walked into the lobby, a few heads turned. Last summer, an acquaintance had said, *Wow, I guess you have to avoid being seen around town with your parents—the optics won't be good.*

Brent had been horrified—that it was both true and that someone thought he'd take that into account. He might not have the same relationship with June and Clifford now that he'd had before six months ago, but he'd never be able to give up on his parents. Never give up on hoping for the better out of both of them.

He followed his dad down to the end of the hall, glad he wasn't on the second floor like Sage. Running into her would be awkward, and he'd have to introduce them—reintroduce them, since they'd met all those years ago, of course. And Brent wanted to keep the focus of this get together on his father.

Inside the room, Clifford headed for the small round table with two chairs by the window. He sat down and took out his lunch, popping open the tab to his soda. Brent let his dad have a few bites before launching into why he was there.

"I assume you're also here to apologize," Clifford said, squeezing ketchup on his fries.

Brent narrowed his eyes. "For what, exactly?"

"For all but accusing me of tampering with the election back in November. That was all JenniLynn's husband's doing."

"And Marty's," Brent reminded him. "Texts were found incriminating both of them."

"But not *me*. And yet even without any evidence, you still didn't believe me when I said I was innocent."

Brent didn't believe his father then and still didn't. Clifford and Marty had been thick as thieves. His dad had much to gain from then acting mayor Marty Moore being elected, such as swaying public opinion of Clifford.

It was possible that his dad hadn't been mixed up in that, but… "I want to believe you didn't have anything to do with it, Dad. But you've done some pretty unethical things."

"And we talked about all that last summer," Clifford said, then took a big bite of his burger. The topic of conversation seemed to have no effect on the man's appetite. Brent, however, felt queasy.

They had talked about the past, Clifford Woodson's terrible actions, Brent demanding answers, his dad coming up with rehearsed politician's platitudes about putting his family above all else. Listening to his father defend his actions, what he'd done to the Deroy family, to Barrett Jr., had been sickening.

"I've been forced to reckon with my…mistakes," Clifford said. "My whole life was turned upside down! And now I'm getting divorced. We stuck by each other for fifteen years—and for what? For nothing!"

You stuck together to protect each other's secrets. Because you two were the only ones who knew what you each did. There had probably been a comfort in that too. And each lording something over the other.

He turned away, the smell of the burger and fries making him feel sicker.

"I did good things for Tenacity in my tenure as mayor," Clifford said, then took a sip of his soda. "But I want you to remember something, Brent. I *saved* this family."

Brent mentally rolled his eyes, trying to keep a hold on his anger. "This again?"

"Damned right," Clifford said, jabbing a finger at Brent. "If I hadn't blackmailed Deroy into leaving, guess what? Your mother would have left with him. Now guess how fast it would have come out that June stole the money, that she ran off with her lover? Our family would have been destroyed. You might have been able to withstand the heat, but not your sister. She was just twelve! A kid. Can you imagine how the gossip and scandal and humiliation would have affected Victoria? Thanks to me, we had fifteen good years before everything got ruined."

Slowly, in his head, Brent counted to five. His father was some piece of work.

And Clifford Woodson had been more focused on *himself* than his children.

"And mark my words, son," his father said, "folks will regret not voting Marty into office. JenniLynn will ruin Tenacity."

Unbelievable. "I think Mayor Garrett will do great things for this town," Brent said. He wasn't going to get anywhere with his father.

"Humph," Cliff said, swiping a fry through ketchup. This conversation didn't seem to have the man breaking a sweat in the slightest. "And even though the statute of limitations ran out on any potential charges against your mother and me, I might as well be in jail for how I'm treated in town—including by my own family."

Someone get out the tiny violins. "Do you feel any remorse for what you did to the Deroys?" Brent crossed his arms over his chest.

"Remorse? I just told you—I *had* to do it!"

His father would skate free the way some Tefloncoated criminals did. And he'd be crying *poor me, woe is me* to whoever would listen.

His father patted his stomach. "I'm so full. I should have gotten the pie, though. The Silver Spur has great pie, you agree? Or do you prefer the ones at Betty's Bakehouse?"

Brent leaned his head back and let out a sigh. "I need to get going, Dad. You take care." *Because I'm not sure when we'll speak next. I'm done here.*

His father stood, a moment of regret on Clifford's face that hinted that he wished he and Brent could be the way they used to be. "If you see your mother, you tell her it was her affair that got us all into this mess. If she hadn't cheated, none of this would have happened. She wouldn't have stolen the money to fund her getaway with her lover. And I wouldn't have had to do what I did to save our family."

Brent looked at his father and felt so heavy hearted, so *awful*, that he had to get out of there. Without another word, he turned and left.

Outside the inn, he gulped in the fresh air, perilously close to tears. He didn't know how he'd ever be close with his father again—not that they'd ever really been close, since his homelife had been a lie. Same with his mother.

Just focus on your relationship with Victoria. Just be grateful the two of you have each other.

With that, he felt better. And better still at the idea of going back inside the hotel to see Sage right now. He needed to be with her. To hold her, to hear her voice.

Sage and their beautiful new relationship was his way forward, his North Star.

He went back inside and up the stairs to the second floor. He knocked on the door to Room 214. And waited, the anticipation alone filling his heart with all good things instead of the dread inside him just a few minutes ago.

But there was no answer. He knocked again. No sounds coming from inside. Darn it—she wasn't here. Disappointment flooded him.

That was how much Sage had come to mean to him, how much he needed her. Their relationship came with complications, but they were forging ahead, in mutual agreement, which meant he could forget everything but how good it would feel to have her in his arms. To hopefully spend the night with her again—and this time not in the gloomy silence of last night. He'd get away from the inn, which right now felt more about his dad than Sage, and he'd call her once he was back on his own turf. A place where everything always made sense—his ranch.

He was about to turn to go back down the stairs when his phone pinged with a text. It was from Sage.

Hey, had a bad day and sitting on your porch, needing a dose of you. Close by?

How simpatico were they?

His heart actually moved in his chest and relief relaxed his shoulders. He was sorry she'd had a cruddy day on top of last night, but to know she was right on his doorstep, needing him too…

I'm standing at the door to your room. I could have written that same text. Be there ASAP.

She sent back a smiley face emoji wearing a cow-boy hat. And a red heart.

His bad mood was replaced by sweet anticipation.

When Sage heard Brent's pickup coming up the drive, she slipped her sketch pad and box of pastels into her tote bag, then stood up, her entire body brimming with relief. After that terrible argument with her parents earlier, she'd driven back to the hotel and paced around her room for a while, then needed to get out. She'd driven around, taking in the town she was going to call home again. She'd done a search on available apartments and homes for rent and sale, and there were a few that caught her interest. Within a half hour of trying to focus on her big decision of moving to Tenacity and living on her own, painting full-time, she'd been restored.

Until she'd happened to be driving past Castillo's and saw her parents walking in for lunch as if everything was just peachy in their world, as if they weren't at odds with their daughter. And then everything that had been said that morning had come flooding back, and she'd been right back where she'd started. Earlier, she hadn't wanted to run to Brent and dump on him, be in his arms for support. But seeing her parents going to lunch as if they weren't tied in knots like she was made her feel terribly lonely.

And so she'd driven out to his ranch. His pickup was gone, so she knew he wasn't there. She'd plopped down on the porch and texted him, needing to see him so badly.

And his response had gone straight into her heart, lifting it up. While waiting for him, she'd pulled out her pastels and sketchbook, her head and heart both soothed.

Now she watched Brent pull in by the fence. When he stepped out of the truck, she ran to him, throwing her arms around him. He held her tightly. Just what she needed. And from his text, what he needed too.

"I have a good idea," she whispered into his ear.

He leaned back a bit and smiled. "Does it involve staying this close to each other?"

"Closer," she said and kissed him.

"Hmm," he teased. "What could this involve?" he asked, taking her hand and heading her up the porch steps. "Am I getting warmer?"

"Oh yes," she said as he opened the door. "In a little farther and to the left."

She followed his gaze to the big stone fireplace, the cozy rug in front of it. She dropped her tote, and they kissed their way over. "Couldn't you go for some hot cocoa? While stretched out in front of a roaring fire? Our minds blessedly blank? No thinking about our obviously equally bad mornings?" Last night, they'd coped by being together physically but apart emotionally, not really talking, not making love. Today they both needed something else.

He pulled her close again. "I only want to think about you. About us."

"Same," she said, lifting up to kiss him. "I'll make the cocoa. You do the fire. And I'll meet you back here."

He kissed her back, and she felt so comforted, so cared for, so happy in this moment that the morning fell away. She found cocoa mix in the cabinet and heated up two mugs of milk, then made a plate of cheese and crackers and red grapes, and brought it in on a tray. The fire was blazing, and Brent was sitting in front of it on the rug, staring into the flames like his bad day had just come roaring back to him.

She set down the tray and sat beside him, handing him a mug. "Hey, you okay?"

"You left for less than two minutes, and my mind wandered, unfortunately." His blue eyes were troubled. Whatever had happened had done a number on him.

"Let's talk about it, then," she said. "Sometimes that's what the doctor ordered instead of trying to forget or sweep it under the rug."

"I think that right now, what I need is to have my mind occupied with something much more pleasant. But if you want to talk about your hard morning, I'm here, Sage. Really."

She took his hand and held it for a moment. "Actually, let's toast to ignoring everything but us, right here, right now." They picked up their mugs and they lightly clinked, then sipped the cocoa. Hot and comforting and sweet. Like Brent.

"How'd you know I needed this?" he asked. "Exactly this."

"I guess we're just in sync," she said. "Like how we each just went to see the other at the same time." She smiled and set down her mug, then fed him a grape.

He fed her a piece of cheddar cheese. "I could do this forever."

A few more nibbles later, he moved his mouth onto her neck. "A little warm for all these clothes," he said, gesturing at the fire.

"I agree. But first—" She popped up and drew the curtains along the long wall of windows that faced the front of the house. Anyone driving up or coming up the porch steps could see in.

He smiled. "Good idea. This is our own private afternoon delight."

She laughed and sank down on her knees in front of him, then unbuttoned his flannel shirt while he pulled off her sweater. She reveled in the way his gaze dropped to her lacy formfitting cami. He slowly took it off, his hands warm on her back.

His intake of breath as her hands landed on his chest made her smile. He pulled her against him and kissed her, so passionately that she felt every cell in her body tighten and then expand. She felt his hand move to the button of her jeans, which he undid. She unbuttoned his. Then they shimmied out of their jeans and socks, Sage in just her bra and underwear, Brent in his sexy black boxer briefs.

She slid a hand under the waistband and dipped it lower, and he sucked in a breath again and let out a grunt as her hand wrapped around him. His entire body stiffened as though he was fighting for control, then he kissed her so passionately that her knees couldn't support her any longer, and she slid her legs out and lay down. Brent moved on top of her, cupping her face with his hands, the tenderness in his eyes, in his expression, telling her everything she needed to know about how he felt about her.

She closed her eyes and felt him inching down her underwear. He must have taken off his, too, because the next thing she knew, he was inside her, gently and then slowly adding pressure until it was she who was about to lose control.

And for the next little while, their mission to forget everything but each other was accomplished.

Chapter Eleven

Sage opened her eyes, her head resting in the nook of Brent's shoulder. He was asleep. She glanced across the room out the side windows; it was still plenty light out, so they must not have dozed for long. Just a perfect little nap for a perfect little afternoon interlude.

She stretched like a cat, content and happy, then snuggled even closer to Brent. Earlier, when she'd been driving around, so upset by her argument with her parents, her mind had gone to worrisome places. That maybe she was reading Brent wrong all over again. That maybe she was just a soft place for him to land. Then she quickly realized she had Bert's and Rosemary's voices in her head. And she shook it all away.

She felt Brent stirring beside her. "I have no idea what time it is," she said. "I just know I needed that. All of it. Including the nap." She shifted onto her side and looked up at him.

He smiled too. "Same. Honestly, right now I feel like nothing can touch me. I went to see my dad—and that conversation is like a distant memory. It'll come roaring back, but right now, it's muted."

"Same here with my parents," she said. Except everything the Abernathys had said suddenly burst into her head in Technicolor. "Ugh, it's back already. So much for the reprieve."

"I'm so sorry, Sage. Tell me what happened."

She inwardly sighed and grabbed her clothes. "I need some armor for this." Sage quickly got dressed, then sat back down, staring at the fire that was dying down. She pulled a ponytail holder from her jeans pocket and quickly braided her hair down her shoulder, securing it.

He got dressed, too, then sat beside her. "Oh no. That bad?"

She nodded and brought her knees up, resting her arms on them. "I told them I made a decision about my life. That I was ready to strike out on my own, have my own place and focus on my art. My dad seemed amenable, but my mother was pretty harsh about it." She shook her head. "Ugh, your turn. I don't want to think about that right now."

"I'm glad to hear your dad's on your side," he said, holding her hand. "Maybe he'll help your mom understand."

"Maybe, but I really don't know. Speaking of dads— did you run into yours or go see him?"

He nodded. "I went to find him. I was thinking about it last night, that it was time to sit down with him and somehow find some peace for myself. I didn't know exactly what I wanted from him, either. He did what he did and there's no way around that. Maybe I just wanted to see that he was sorry. That he wanted to at least try to fix his relationship with me and Victoria. Instead, he rambled on about how everything he did was for his family. That if he hadn't blackmailed Deroy, his own family would have been humiliated, especially my sister." He shook his head. "Like he cared about anyone but himself. Please."

Her heart ached for him. "Oh, Brent, I'm really sorry. I know you haven't spoken to your dad in a couple of months and were hoping time would help."

"And it didn't. He's the same man he was fifteen years ago when he got away with something heinous. The same man he was six months ago when his manipulations were uncovered."

"You're not the same," she said. "It's probably why talking to him is so impossible."

"Exactly. You know what I can't get over? That there had to be more going on than I was even aware of. And that I'll never know because the truth is being withheld. Little things. There's just some stuff that doesn't make sense." He threw up his hands. "I should just forget about it. Let it all go and try to move on."

But he couldn't. Because things weren't settled. Because he still had questions.

And *she* had some answers.

Her heart started beating a little too fast as anxiety gripped her. She sucked in a breath. She had to tell him. All this man wanted was honesty. From his family. From himself. And *she* was going to withhold what she knew? What she *believed*?

There were two things she knew back then that he didn't. One was about his mother. The other, she'd only had a piece of—but the startling truth had become clear to Sage when she arrived in town and learned what his parents had done to the Deroys. Things she hadn't understood in the past made sense now.

She'd start with what he *did* know, with what was public knowledge now. "Brent, I'd like to ask you something. About your mother's affair."

"Okay," he said, leaning to press a kiss to her temple.

She inwardly winced. In about thirty seconds, he might want to take that kiss back. Might want to take back their entire reunion and new romance.

"You didn't hear the gossip that your mom was having an affair fifteen years ago?" she asked. "I don't mean with Barrett Sr.—no one knew it was him back then. But there *was* gossip that she was stepping out on her marriage."

"I never heard gossip about my mother, period. I would have beat up anyone who dared say she was cheating on my dad." He winced. "Duh, maybe that's why I never did hear anything. But are you saying you heard the gossip?"

She closed her eyes for a second. "Yes. I heard it. But at first, it was just that. Gossip, right? So it never occurred to me to bring it up with you."

He seemed relieved at that. "Right. Completely agree. Apparently, everyone thought she was cheating with the man who drove the ice cream truck. Cheetah or Cheeto or something."

"Cheeto," she said.

"Well, everyone turned out to be wrong about *who*," he said. "She *was* having an affair, though—with Barrett Deroy Sr."

"I know," she said and sucked in another breath. "I know because fifteen years ago, I saw them kissing one night."

He gasped and turned to her. "*What?*"

Okay, truth number one. "I had dinner at a girl-friend's house and was headed home. It was dark and foggy out, and I cut through the Town Hall parking lot. I saw your mom and Barrett Deroy Sr. kissing in a back doorway facing the woods. Just a week before the Deroys left town."

He was staring at her, confusion and something else she couldn't quite identify in his expression. "Why didn't you tell me?"

"I was afraid to tell you. Afraid of hurting you with such shocking news. Afraid that I misread what I saw. Afraid of saying something and being called a liar— by you or by your mother. By the time I got home that night, I was so confused that I wasn't even sure I did see them kiss. I convinced myself that it was so dark and foggy that maybe I'd been mistaken."

"Except you weren't," he said, his voice flat, devoid of emotion. "You know what you saw."

She nodded slowly. "I absolutely saw them passion-ately kissing. There was no mistaking it. I just wanted to be wrong, Brent. And then around a week later, my family ended up moving away."

His face was pale, his eyes so conflicted. "If you'd told me, if I'd confronted my mother, she might have stopped the affair—for her kids' sake. She would have dropped the whole plan to run away with Bar-rett Sr. She wouldn't have stolen the money. My father wouldn't have blackmailed the Deroys. This whole damned thing wouldn't have *happened*."

Now it was Sage's turn to gasp. Was all that true? Could she have prevented everything just by telling him what she'd seen? Tears stung her eyes. "Brent, I—" She stopped talking, the tears streaming now.

He closed his eyes for a second and breathed in, then opened his eyes and looked at her. He shook his head. "No. I'm wrong. Completely wrong. What happened wasn't your fault. I can't even believe I even said all that. My mother had an affair. And wrong or right of me to say, I believe in my heart that my father drove her to it. They're both wrong. And then my father set a despicable plan into motion. It's *their* fault."

Her heart stopped pounding, breath coming back into her lungs.

Brent stood up and walked over to the windows, pulling back the curtains slightly to look out. He seemed to be thinking. Or trying to calm himself down. Then he turned back. "You were fifteen and scared. Of course you didn't say anything about seeing my mom and Deroy. You didn't even know about the aftermath till you came back to town. And even if you *had* told me back then, if I *had* confronted my mom, she might have still stolen the money and planned to run off with him. Who knows?" He came back and sat beside her, taking her hands. "I'm sorry I blamed you for even a second just before."

Relief poured through her. She'd been wanting to get that off her chest for a long time. "That means so much to me, Brent."

Except there was more. Something that wasn't public knowledge. Something she knew and he didn't.

And if she withheld it, if it came out later—and it possibly would, because someone very close to him knew it too—it would break his heart. And change how he felt about Sage, how he saw her. He'd never forgive her.

"Brent," she said, hearing her voice shaking, "there's something else I should tell you. Something from back then."

He turned to her and waited. Right now, his expression wasn't tense. He wasn't expecting a bombshell. How she wished they could stay this way.

She sucked in a breath and reached for his hands again. "It's about the money your mother stole from Town Hall."

He tilted his head. "What about it?"

"You've always wondered why your mother never returned it after the whole plot to run away was derailed. Why she'd let everyone believe Barrett Jr. had taken the money. You said she was evasive about it but that she figured your dad found it and hid it. He denied it, though."

He nodded. "I believed him on that. Since the truth came out, I usually can tell when he's lying. I figure it must have been my mom. She hid the money instead of returning it because she felt she didn't have a choice, really. If she'd put it back, people would start asking questions, like why a thief whose family fled would return thousands of dollars. I don't know."

"I do," she said, so quietly she wasn't sure he heard.

He stared hard at her. "What do you mean?"

Say it, she ordered herself. *Just say it*. "The reason your mother never returned the money was that it *disappeared*. Someone else in your family found the money and secretly hid it under that boulder at the Juniper Road property."

"Someone else? I just told you—my dad didn't do it."

"I'm not talking about your father, Brent." Sage closed her eyes for a second. She did not want to see Brent's expression when she said what would follow. But she had to be honest here. And accept what was coming.

"Well, there is no one else, Sage. So I don't know what you're—" He stopped speaking and stared at her quizzically. "My mother told me that after she stole the money, she stashed it in her bedroom. The only other people in our house were me and Victoria. I didn't hide the money and there's no way it was my then twelve-year-old sister—"

"I think it *was* Victoria," Sage said quietly.

He slipped his hands from hers and crossed his arms over his chest, shifting over a few inches. He faced her now on the rug, his expression not quite stony, but hard nonetheless. "Why would you *possibly* think that?"

There was no turning back now.

What the hell was going on here? Brent's head felt like it was stuffed with cotton and he couldn't think straight. Sage was saying she thought his sister found the money and then hid it?

Sage was quiet, staring down at the floor, then out the windows. She looked nervous—and upset.

But mostly sad.

She looked at him, her expression so troubled. "That summer we were dating, sometimes I'd get to your house early while waiting for you to get home from football practice, and Victoria would invite me to her room.

"She began confiding to me about little things, then bigger things. I was a few years older and I guess she trusted me, felt comfortable sharing with me. She said your parents were arguing a lot and that she hated it. And sometimes she'd hear your mom whispering on the phone and giggling."

"Whispering to who?" A girlfriend? A relative? Her lover? His blood went cold as he understood what Sage was saying. No. No way. Victoria was twelve. If she'd overheard his mom talking to Barrett Sr. on the phone, she wouldn't have understood they were having an affair. Come on.

"She never said. But…after I saw her and Barrett Sr. kissing, I realized she must have overheard the two of them. I don't know, though."

"So conjecture," he said, his arms tightening over his chest. "You assumed."

She looked down for a moment and then nodded. "When I came back to Tenacity and heard what happened to the Deroys, things started filling in. I think your sister overheard your mom and Barrett Deroy Sr. talking on the phone about their plan to run off together. That she had the money tucked away safe. And I think Victoria either went looking for it—or just found it and knew what it was. So she took the money and she hid it where no one would ever find it. To stop your mother from running away with her lover."

He shook his head. "You got all that from my sister telling you she heard our mom giggling on the phone? Please, Sage. What the hell?"

"It's more than just that, Brent. When I look back now on all the things your sister said—about a secret she had, about finding something, about how people could shock you—she was always vague and then quickly changed the subject, and I thought she was talking about school stuff, friend stuff. I had no idea your mother had very recently stolen money from the town. No one did except for two people. Your dad and—I think— Victoria."

Brent did what he always did when he was angry and needed to calm down. He mentally counted to five. Then again. "How could you, Sage?"

She was staring at him, her brown eyes wide, her hands shaky.

"How could you point fingers at my sister? After all she's been through? Victoria was twelve back then. *Twelve.* You do realize what you are saying, right? That my sister *knew* Barrett was innocent and never said a word in his absence while everyone thought he was a thief? Back then and all these years later? Even when the truth came out, she still said nothing? Come on, Sage. You can't believe that."

"I do believe it," she said. "And because I do, I had to tell you. You've been lied to for so many years by the people closest to you, people you love dearly. I couldn't keep this secret from you."

As the roar in his chest was louder than how hard his heart was pounding, he brought the palms of his hands to the sides of his head. This was *insane*. "I don't want to say anything I'll regret—tomorrow or fifty years from now, so I'm just going to ask you to leave, Sage."

After that talk with his dad in his hotel room earlier, he'd thought the day couldn't possibly get worse. It had in ways he'd never could have imagined, not even with his eyes wide open the past six months. Aware, non-self-absorbed, Brent 2.0. He'd never have thought this kind of betrayal from Sage Abernathy possible—for reasons he couldn't fathom either—.

Tears slipped down Sage's cheeks. "Brent, please— let's talk about this."

"There's nothing to talk about. You've said it all, right? And trust me, I know that people see what they want to see, believe what they want to believe. You're no different. Please go."

The tears streamed harder down her cheeks. She grabbed her tote bag and rushed toward the door, pulling on her coat and boots. Her hand on the doorknob, she turned back. "I'm sorry, Brent."

"You know, Sage. I used to think Victoria was all I had until you came back into my life. But right now, I realize she *is* all I have. And that makes what you're accusing her of even more painful."

"Please, Brent," she said, her voice cracking. "Let me—"

He held up a hand. "We're done here, Sage."

Her tears fell even harder, but he felt so hollow he wasn't moved. She was staring, her red-rimmed eyes pleading with him.

He said nothing and she opened the door and left, shutting it behind her.

He closed his eyes, a pain gripping his chest so intensely that he had to sit down in the chair by the fireplace. He'd thought his heart was broken six months ago? He'd had no idea what pain felt like.

Chapter Twelve

Brent wasn't even sure how he got through the next hour on the ranch. He'd had to get out of the house, away from where Sage had taken his heart out of his chest and crushed it in her bare hands.

Dramatic? Maybe. But that was how it had felt.

Betrayed by the woman he loved.

His little sister, forever his little sis, accused of something awful. Because of vague "little things" his sister had said fifteen years ago. Things that didn't add up to what Sage was insistent Victoria had done. With no actual evidence.

This was exactly how some people had been treating him since last summer. He'd never have expected that from Sage—the woman he'd felt so close to. The woman he'd spent such intense, passionate times with. The past few days, he'd been able to feel the cracks in his heart filling.

Now all those raw places inside him felt liked they'd been packed with fresh salt—and rubbed hard.

After Sage had left, Brent had stalked around the ranch, avoiding his employees since he didn't want to bite anyone's head off, and he was that upset. A hand had texted he was feeling sick and needed to leave early, and Brent had texted back no problem, since taking over the guy's duties had been perfect for Brent's mood. Physical labor—raking dirty straw, maneuvering a wheelbarrow full of fresh bedding—would distract him.

It hadn't. By the time he'd finished three pens, his head felt like it might explode. The ranch work gave him too much time to think. And that was the last thing he wanted to do.

At four thirty he was supposed to meet Barrett at the home gym his partner created in the basement of his ranch house; they were having a workout meeting to catch up on where things stood for the foundation so that they could be prepared for a bigger meeting tomorrow with Seth Taylor to go over numbers and the spreadsheets. But Brent couldn't face Barrett Deroy today—not with what Sage had suggested his sister had done burning in his gut.

He couldn't imagine going anywhere or doing anything—particularly anything requiring focus. Besides, if Brent even tried to lift a weight right now, he'd end up dropping it on his foot. His concentration was shot and he wasn't himself.

He'd go down a beer at the Grizzly and get himself centered, then call Barrett and let him know he couldn't come over today but maybe they could hook up an hour before the meeting with Seth tomorrow. That was Brent's plan. A beer, then home for a long, hot shower and letting everything just settle, and surely he'd feel at least a drop better.

Except when he got to the Grizzly, glad to see the place wasn't busy—which, given the hour wasn't unusual—one beer hadn't been enough. So he'd had another. Then another. And then he forgot what day it was. Maybe *that* had been the plan all along.

"You okay, Woodson?" asked the big, burly bartender, Grizzly owner Dale Clutterbuck. "Should I cut you off?"

"Yes," said a familiar male voice from behind Brent.

"Copy that," Dale said, stroking his beard.

Brent turned and sighed. Dammit.

Barrett Deroy stood there in his barn coat and the cowboy hat Brent had given him for his last birthday, tapping his watch. "Forget our meeting?"

"No. I just couldn't deal with it."

Barrett looked at him quizzically. "Why not?"

"I don't want to talk about it." A country tune about love gone wrong came on the jukebox, and Brent scowled harder.

"You'd just rather drink your troubles away," Barrett said, sitting on the stool beside Brent. He turned to Dale, who was now drying glasses a few feet down the bar. "We'll take two coffees, if you have a pot going."

"Always do," Dale said, heading farther down the bar. Sobering people up was a necessity at a place like the Grizzly.

"How'd you know where to find me, anyway?" Brent asked.

"Very small town. I was about to head to your place to see if you fell off a hay bale or something and was out cold and needing medical attention when I spotted your truck out front."

Brent sighed again. "Can't hide in Tenacity, that's for sure."

"You trying to?" Barrett asked, taking off his hat and running a hand through his brown hair. He set the Stetson on the stool beside him.

Brent shrugged, staring at rows of liquor on the shelves behind the bar. Dale was back with two mugs of coffee, one with a Strom and Son Feed and Farm Supply logo, the other a Grizzly one with faded lettering. He set down a silver pitcher of creamer and some sugar packets.

Barrett fixed both their coffees; he'd met with Brent enough times to know how he took his coffee, and the *I know you* gesture softened something inside Brent. Deroy was the *last* person Brent wanted to be with right now. But the one person who'd understand. Of course, Brent couldn't tell him anything, though.

Why would Sage have said all that? Suggested that? Believed any of that? he kept thinking, aware he was kind of drunk. *How dare she?* He shook his head, tossing the little brown plastic stir stick on the bar.

"Let me guess," Barrett said. "I could come up with a few reasons why you might be in the Grizzly at five in the afternoon instead of at my place, lifting weights and talking numbers. But I'm gonna put my money on woman troubles. You and Sage got into an argument."

You don't know the half of it, Brent thought. He grunted and got a compassionate nod. "I don't want to talk about."

Barrett nodded and took a long sip of his coffee, so Brent did too. The hot brew was more comforting than he expected, but he wasn't looking to be more alert. Less would be fine.

"Okay," Barrett said. "We don't have to talk about that. We can talk about another couple's problems. I got a call from my mom today."

Brent was glad he'd changed the subject. Not that he wanted to hear whatever was coming next out of his friend's mouth. Talking about *any* of this right now was hard.

Maybe if Brent didn't comment, Barrett would talk sports instead.

"The divorce will be final next week," Barrett said. "I know their marriage has been over for a long time but it still stings."

Brent glanced at him, suddenly too concerned about his friend to hope that being silent would lead to only small talk. "I hear you. My parents aren't far behind in their own divorce."

Barrett slugged down some coffee. "The whole thing is just sad, right? All around. My mother gave it her all, but once the dust settled, she knew she had to leave, that there was no fixing what was that broken."

That was exactly how Brent felt about his own parents' marriage. Broken. He supposed irrevocably.

"My mom said it took her a long time to process that her own husband knew I was innocent of the theft and didn't tell her," Barrett added. "He'd let her think her son was guilty all those years so that she wouldn't find out about his affair with your mom."

"Damn," Brent said. "And then it all came out publicly. You know, these past six months, I didn't even stop to think about how your mom's life was changed back then, thinking the worst about her child. And then fifteen years later, learning—along with everyone else—about her husband's affair and the plan to run away." Brent wasn't surprised that Macy Deroy had taken off for an artist colony months ago.

Barrett nodded. "She was blindsided. And then felt really, really dumb. The good news is that the two of us have gotten closer. My father and I are another story. I'll always love him—I don't have to tell *you* how that goes—but I can't forget what he did to me—what he *allowed* to happen to me even if he thought he was saving me from being framed. He could have spoken up."

"We know why he didn't," Barrett said. "And that must have burned your mother's gut even worse."

Brent let out a hard sigh. "Because he knew if he fought for me, he'd destroy his lover's life with the truth. She'd have gone to jail where we'd been offered the chance to flee and start new lives." He shook his head. "No matter how I look at it, I'm always forced back to square one. That it was a mess."

Brent's stomach churned with just how true that was. Fifteen years ago. Six months ago. And now. Still. It kept coming back, making problems.

Sage's beautiful face came to his mind and he blinked it away—hard. He was tipsy enough that tears would start poking his eyes if he let himself think about her. And all she'd said.

"Refill?" Dale asked, coming over with the coffeepot.

"Shot of whiskey," Barrett said, then held up a hand. "Just kidding. Yes on the caffeine refill."

Brent held up his empty mug. "Same." After Dale poured and left, Brent said, "I have a really dumb question for you." He shook his head. "Nah, forget it. I can't even bear to ask."

"We can both take it," Barrett said. "We've been *through* it. So shoot."

"Okay. What do you think holidays are going to be like? Christmas with one, Easter with the other? What about when you and Nina have kids? Will your children ever see their nana and pop-pop in the same room?" He shook his head. "I guess I'm wondering for myself, not that marriage and kids is in my future." He winced, surprised he'd said that. He didn't want to talk about Sage.

Barrett eyed him. "I don't know. I guess I'm hoping my folks will put aside their past for the sake of their grandkids. For me and Nina. And get through all family celebrations just fine."

Brent thought of Victoria, how much it would mean to her to see her parents in the same room without them glaring at each other or screeching. "My parents were both stubborn about not leaving the family house, but things came to a head and my dad finally moved out this week into the Tenacity Inn at the monthly rate. I think the next time they'll be in the same room together is when their divorce is finalized and they get the decree."

"Personally, I think they should take a cue from my mom and her artist's colony—do some serious deep thinking—separately. A month-long silent retreat in the mountains where they go hiking and drink green juice. Or some self-help podcasts."

That actually managed to make Brent laugh, and he held out his mug. "I will toast to that truth."

Barrett smiled and clinked, and both downed the rest of their refills. "So...want some advice?"

"I don't know if I do."

"Well, it's free," Barrett said, "so here it is. I know you said you don't want to talk about it, but whatever's going on with you and Sage, whatever got you in this bar, *don't* give up on your relationship."

So Barrett had caught that bit about Brent not getting married or having kids any time soon. But he still *didn't* want to talk about it. He couldn't, anyway.

"Love—real love—is hard to come by, Brent. I *know*. After what the two of us have been through, when you find someone that special, and someone truly honest who you can trust, grab them and never let them go."

Honest. Trust. Brent mentally shook his head. He'd thought he'd had that in Sage until this afternoon. Till one *Here's what I think* ripped it all apart and away.

And in the guise of being honest. Of not keeping secrets. Right. Damn, he was bitter now.

"Deroy, where is *your* bitterness? How can you be this okay?" Brent had asked him that more than a few times the past six months. But he never understood. He still didn't.

"It helps that I love someone with everything I am," Barrett said. "That I believe in her love for me. I can't tell you how that changed me, Brent. It filled up cracks, fixed broken places. So don't take it for granted. That's what I want to say most of all, I guess. Don't take it for granted."

Brent grunted. "I could use that shot of whiskey, after all."

"You could use a ride home, actually. Come on, friend. Gimme your keys and I'll drop off your truck later. Nina will follow me and drive me back in her car."

Brent nodded. As he got in the passenger seat of Barrett's vehicle and yanked on the seat belt, his friend's words echoed in his head. *I believe in her love for me…*

Well, Brent *didn't* believe in Sage's love for him. Not that she'd ever said she did, but he'd thought they were heading in that direction. As he'd woken up from the after-sex nap with Sage snuggled against him this afternoon, he'd felt so much for her. And he was under the impression it was mutual.

How could she have strong feelings for him and suggest such a terrible version of the truth? With *no* evidence. When his sister was all he had left of his family. Or it felt like that, anyway.

They were silent on the way to the ranch, Brent staring grumpily out the window. When they pulled up, Barrett insisted on walking him in.

"As a favor for getting you home safely and in one piece," Barrett said on the porch, "do something for me, okay?"

"What's that?" Brent asked.

"I know you said you don't want to talk about Sage

and whatever happened there. But deal with whatever came between you two."

Brent scowled. "I don't want to."

"Yeah, obviously. But you have to. And you owe me, so…"

He did owe Barrett Deroy. A lot. "I'll deal with it," he said. He wasn't sure how, exactly.

As Barrett turned and jogged down the porch steps, he realized his friend was right. Brent *did* have to deal with this. Because he couldn't spend the next twenty years downing beers in the Grizzly and muttering about being betrayed by the woman he thought was on his side.

Somehow, he would deal with it.

Tomorrow, though. For tonight, he'd have a good dinner, take that long, hot shower, and hit the hay early to sleep off the bad mood and the beers, if the caffeine rush would let him. Then, with a fresh brain and a new day, he'd figure things out. *How*, he thought as he shut the door behind him, was beyond him at the moment.

The next morning, Sage stood at the window in her room at the Tenacity Inn, absently nursing the now-cold take-out coffee she'd gotten from the Silver Spur an hour ago. It was close to ten, but she still hadn't eaten anything. Even the delicious-looking muffins in the display at the café hadn't done anything to give her an appetite.

She'd called Brent last night, but he hadn't picked up. She hadn't known what she was going to say beyond, *Can we please talk about this? I'm heartsick over how things ended.* She texted him exactly that, but he didn't respond. When she woke up just before 6:00 a.m., she'd grabbed her phone to see if he'd texted back. Nothing.

And now, as if to ensure she felt even worse, her mother had called five minutes ago to say she was coming up to talk. Sage had no doubt this stalemate would end like the one with Brent.

There was a tap on her door, and Sage went to let her mom in. Rosemary Abernathy stood on the threshold holding a bag from Betty's Bakehouse, her expression neutral. Not at all contrite or sheepish or sorry for the way they'd left things.

Until she peered closely at Sage, tilting her head. Now her mother looked kind of worried. "Are you okay, honey? I mean, I know things were tense yesterday, but you look like you're on the verge of tears."

Sage couldn't help it; the waterworks started. She stood there and sobbed, covering her face with her hands.

Her mother gasped and set down the bag on the desk, then pulled Sage into a hug. And despite not feeling particularly warm and fuzzy toward her mother, a hug was exactly what Sage needed right now.

She pulled back and grabbed some tissues from the box on the bedside table. Dropping down on the edge of the bed, she dabbed at her eyes, trying to get a hold of herself.

"Sage? Is it the argument from yesterday?" her mom asked, sitting beside her.

Sage shook her head. "Well, I mean, I am upset about that. But no."

"You look…heartbroken, honey. Is it Brent? Did you two have a fight?"

Sage started crying again, dropping her face in her hands.

Her mother again pulled her into a hug. "I'm so sorry. Do you want to talk about what happened?" Now her mom pulled back, her expression hardening. "Wait—did he break up with you? Because we're not investing? Humph! I should called that one. Just wait till your father hears about this. He'll read that man the riot act! How dare he—"

Sage held up a hand. "Mom, I didn't even tell Brent you and Dad aren't going to invest. It was…something else."

Rosemary looked surprised. "Oh. But you seemed so happy yesterday, so sure of things between you and Brent. Like you were a united front. Despite my feelings about his…situation, I thought long and hard about that after you left. I thought about *everything*."

Now Sage was the one who was surprised. "You did?"

Her mother nodded and took in a breath. "I'm proud of you, Sage. I always have been."

Sage raised an eyebrow. She wasn't sure she believed that.

It was clear from her mother's expression that she knew it too. "I *am* proud, honey. I've been demanding of you and you've always fulfilled what I thought were your daughterly duties. Working for the ranch. Living at home since you weren't married anyway. Putting family first. I've been so proud of that. But maybe that wasn't so fair of me. To be proud of you for giving up so much of yourself. Who you *are*."

Sage gasped. Was she still fast asleep and dreaming? That couldn't have come out of Rosemary Abernathy's mouth, could it? She gave herself a surreptitious pinch on the back of her arm. It hurt, so she was wide awake.

"When Dad and I got back to the hotel yesterday, and I had some time to sit and think about all that had come up, I started realizing a few things."

"Like what?" Sage asked, still working through her amazement.

"Like how remarkable it was that you defended Brent," her mother said. "I started thinking about what a tough spot he's been in since his family's dirty laundry was aired. If he truly didn't know what his parents had done, the deal his father had struck with Barrett Sr., then my goodness, that poor guy. To have his entire life turned upside down through no doing of his own. To lose his standing in town. To have people think the worst of him. The way your father and I did."

Sage stared at her mom. "Are you saying you've changed your mind about Brent?"

"I'm saying that if *you* believe in him, that's good enough for me and Dad."

Sage's eyes filled with tears again—but this time, from being overwhelmed with *good* emotion. "You have no idea how much that means to me, Mom. No idea."

"I think I do. Like I said, I've been demanding. Now I want to make *you* proud of *me*, Sage."

Sage gasped. "What do you mean?"

"I mean, you have my blessing to go off on your own and live your dream. And I'm sorry for holding you back for so long. I didn't understand before last night, honey."

"Dad talked your ear off, didn't he?" Sage asked with a smile.

"He had something to do with getting me to open my very closed mind. And when I woke up this morning, I knew he was right. And because I love you, because I'm proud of you—everything you are—because I know you, I also know that you wouldn't be in love with a man who doesn't deserve our belief in him. And Seth Taylor and Barrett Jr. wouldn't be working him, either. So after Dad and I sit down tonight to talk numbers, we plan to let Seth know tomorrow that we *will* be investing in the dinosaur park."

"Oh, Mom," she said, wrapping Rosemary into a fierce hug. "I'm so happy to hear you say that. Even though Brent and I are broken up. The dinosaur park is going to completely change Tenacity."

But would Sage even get to see that change? Now that she and Brent were over, maybe she wouldn't move here after all. Could she live in such a small town like Tenacity when the man she loved—her first love— was here?

Maybe she'd check out options for buying and renting in Cheyenne. Or somewhere in between the two places.

"Honey, I thought you and Brent just had an argument—you two broke up?" her mom asked gently.

"What could have possibly happened? Everything was fine yesterday, right?"

Sage recalled how they'd both had bad mornings, had both needed each other. He'd gone to her hotel; she'd gone to his ranch. Her heart clenched at how in sync they'd been. And the way they'd clung to each other, making love in front of the fire, both of them feeling so good afterward, so supported.

And then...

"He's going through a rough time with his family, as you know. And I brought up some things that cut him to the quick. I don't think he'll be able to forgive me."

Her mom seemed to take that in. "Just know this, Sage. If *I* can come around, anyone can."

Sage actually managed to laugh and hugged her mother again, overcome with love and gratitude for this woman. "I appreciate that. But I think it's really over."

"Well, if that changes anything about us investing, just say the word."

Sage shook her head. "Of course not. Two completely different things. *Please* invest—and generously."

Rosemary nodded. "You want to come spend the day with me and Dad? We were planning on attending a livestock auction. We're thinking about adding some Nubian goats."

"Aw, I love goats. But I think what I need to do today is go home—to Cheyenne. At the very least, I'll start packing up my room. And make some decisions about where I'm going to live."

The word *home* echoed in Sage's head. Cheyenne

had never really been home. But could Tenacity be now? She wasn't sure of anything at the moment.

"Sounds like a plan," Rosemary said, standing up. She pointed to the bag. "I got you your favorite kind of croissant—almond. And a blueberry muffin. And a sausage, egg, and cheese on a biscuit in case you didn't have breakfast."

Sage grinned. "I love you, Mom. And tell Dad thank you."

Her mom's eyes sparked. "I will."

With that, her mom left and Sage fell back on the bed and stared up at the ceiling, wondering what on earth had just happened. Somehow, in one of the worst moments of her life, her mother had fixed their relationship and made her believe in possibilities again.

Except when it came to Brent. Sage had a terrible feeling that was over and done. For good.

She couldn't go to him and take back what she'd said. Or apologize for speaking her truth, speaking from her heart. For not having secrets. Sage *did* believe that Victoria Woodson found that money in her mother's bedroom and hid it all those years ago under that boulder at the old property. Victoria had been twelve and scared that her mother would run off with another man. Sage didn't blame her for what she'd done. Even if Victoria did at some point realize the repercussions, the Deroys had left town. Barrett wasn't going to be charged for theft; it was all rumors anyway. The incident was going to be swept under the ole rug.

But there might be repercussions *now* for the fact that when Victoria became an adult, she still hadn't said anything about the money—or returned it to the town. And when the truth had come out six months ago, Victoria had *remained* quiet.

Not that Brent even believed his sister had hidden the money, but if he entertained the idea as a possibility, he'd worry himself sick at what might happen if that news became public.

What a mess. She wrapped her arms around herself, suddenly cold and feeling very alone. She got up and checked her phone again, just in case she somehow missed a ping alerting her to a text.

But not a word from Brent. And she had a feeling she wouldn't be hearing from him.

She grabbed her suitcase and started packing her things, her heart so heavy she could topple over.

Chapter Thirteen

By noon, Brent was ready for a break from both his work on the ranch and his mind churning about all Sage had said yesterday—and about their breakup. He'd called Victoria earlier this morning to ask her over for lunch. Spending some time with his sister would help get his head straight.

That would be *sort of* dealing with things, and he could assure Barrett later today at their meeting with Seth that he was on it. He owed his friend a thank-you for being there for him at Grizzly's, for not judging—as usual—and driving him home. He'd woken up to find his truck in his drive, as promised. But he hadn't even been aware that Barrett and Nina had dropped it off last night; he'd been sleeping off those beers and the headache and heartache, and hadn't even heard them pull in or leave.

Now, as he headed from the barn to the house, he stopped to peer in the pickup's window to look for the keys—they were in the console. Along with a folded-up piece of paper. He opened the door and grabbed the keys, shoving them in his pocket, then read the note.

Remember what I said—don't give up on your relationship. Don't give up on love.

That wrenched a hard sigh out of him. And reminded him suddenly of another note.

One left fifteen years ago with that stolen bunch of cash under the fake boulder at the old property. *You've got the wrong man.*

He shook his head. According to Sage, Victoria was the one who put the money there. And therefore *she* was the one who'd written that note. It had been typed, so no handwriting to analyze. But, come on—a twelve-year-old had actually overheard whispered conversations her mother had had on the phone with her lover, knew about the plan for them to run away, clearly heard about the money June had stolen and either came upon it or went looking for it. Then found it and hid it to thwart the plan.

And given the timing, Clifford must have simultaneously discovered the affair and plan, too, because for Victoria to have written that note—*You've got the wrong man*—she had to have overheard that her father intended to pin the blame on Barrett Deroy Jr.

So a twelve-year-old had done all that?

And who was the *right* man? Their dad?

When the note had been found six months ago, many people thought the right man was Brent himself. That *he'd* hidden the money there to let his rival Barrett Deroy Jr.'s name be turned to mud.

Brent had no idea what that note meant. But he did know Victoria wasn't behind it. If she'd been his age—or even older, actually—maybe he could see all this as a possibility. But come on.

His chest ached at all Sage had suggested. All she'd blown up with one terrible accusation. After all he'd been through, why would she do this to him?

He knew why: because she *believed* every word of the story she'd told him yesterday. And because she didn't want secrets between them. Especially concerning the mess with the families—and his family, in particular. He knew Sage, knew her heart. She wouldn't have told him if she didn't truly believe his sister had found the stolen money and had hidden it with that note.

You've got the wrong man.

He stared at the note Barrett had left in his truck, his chest tightening for his friend. He wanted to do right by Barrett, take his advice, but he couldn't under these circumstances.

Don't give up on your relationship. Don't give up on love.

Well, love had given up on *him*. So what could Brent do about it? Nothing.

He slammed the truck's door shut and leaned against it, feeling all the fight go out of him. He was back to square one here—that Sage was *wrong*. Wrong for believing it in the first place. She had no proof, no evidence, just "little things that added up." Just speculation. He was furious all over again.

At the sound of a car driving up, he took in a deep breath and squared his shoulders. Victoria was here. He'd have lunch with his sister and feel okay again because at least he had Victoria, and no matter what, they'd be each other's family, just the two of them. And he'd somehow move on, keep going, focus on the foundation and the town.

He walked toward her as she exited her car, the sight of his sister, her long, dark hair in a ponytail, her vintage oversize wool coat—no doubt from Nothin' New—the consignment store where she worked—obscuring her slender frame, brightening his mood. She smiled and waved with her mittened hand.

But as he approached, her smile faded.

She studied him, tilting her head. "Uh-oh. Something happened. You look really upset, Brent."

He stared at her, kind of dumbfounded. "I look like I always do."

"Nope. I can see something's bothering you. I notice things. It's not a gift, trust me. Sometimes I wish I didn't see so much. I assume it's about seeing Dad yesterday?"

He was stuck on what she'd said a second ago. That she noticed things. He'd always known she was a sensitive soul. But could she have noticed more than he could ever have thought at only twelve years old? *Had* she known about the affair and plan and blackmail?

He mentally shook his head. No way.

"Well, you *are* good at reading people, because I'm pretty shaken up. About Dad, yes, and what a bust going to see him was. But it's more than that."

"What happened?" she asked, concern on her face.

"Let's go in," he said. "Turkey BLTs, like old times?"

She gave a weak smile. "Sounds great." As they

walked up the porch steps, she stopped and touched his arm. "Oh no, Brent, is it Sage? Are you guys in a fight or something?"

He wasn't sure he wanted to talk about it. He *couldn't* talk about it. But the burning pit in his gut was growing hotter.

They headed in and he shut door behind them, both taking off their coats and boots. The more he looked at his sister—sweet Victoria, innocent in the whole mess—the angrier he felt at all Sage had said.

"We broke up. And if you knew why, what she'd suggested about you—" He clamped his mouth shut, mentally kicking himself. Why the hell had he said that? He hadn't been planning on telling Victoria what Sage had said. What would be the point?

Dammit. He had to work on his reactions. He couldn't go around blurting things out. He was supposed to be putting others first, and instead he'd just blindsided his own sister. Just because he was upset.

Victoria froze in the foyer. "What she suggested about *me*?" She turned to him, her face paler, her dark eyes probing. "What did she say?"

Brent shook his head. "It doesn't matter, Vick. We broke up, we're done, and I need to put it behind me in order to move on, right?" He sucked in a deep breath. "Barbecue potato chips, or salt and vinegar?" he asked, trying to inject a lighter tone into his voice.

Victoria bit her lip and walked into the kitchen, sitting down at the table. "Please tell me, Brent. It clearly is about me."

He went to the refrigerator and took out the turkey,

bacon, and lettuce, setting them on the counter, then grabbed the loaf of sourdough and found a tomato. He opened the fridge again, looking around. "Where's the mayo hiding? Why is this fridge so full?"

Victoria stood up. "Brent."

He stopped and closed his eyes for a second, that ache back in his chest. He closed the refrigerator and walked over to the table and sat down. Victoria sat too.

"Okay. Sage had some crazy notion that *you* were the one who'd hidden the stolen money at the old property." He rolled his eyes. "Come on."

Victoria looked stricken. She was quiet for a moment. Then looked at him and said, "And you broke up because of that?"

"Of course," he said. "How dare she suggest such a thing? After all you and I have been through with Mom and Dad? With the town? You're my *sister*, Victoria. And you're the only family I really have—at least, it feels that way."

Victoria stared from him to the tabletop, her hand slowly moving to the region of her heart. She was clearly deeply hurt.

"And for Sage to say the whole reason she even told me," he continued, "was because she couldn't bear to withhold the truth from me? That honesty was everything and there couldn't be secrets between us? Vick, that she could even *think* you had something to do with all that back then." He shook his head. "I never would have thought that Sage could—"

Victoria looked up at him, holding his gaze, tears in her eyes, so he stopped speaking. She'd clearly had enough. He could see his sister was very upset and got up to hug her, but she held up a hand. "Brent. It's true. It's all true."

He froze, then felt off-balance and dropped back onto the chair. He stared at his sister, unable to process what he'd just heard. "What? You're saying you *did* hide the money at the old property?"

She slowly nodded, tears dripping down her cheeks. She wiped them away. "I heard Mom whispering on the phone to someone. She sounded so happy, Brent. I hadn't heard her sound like that in a long time. I was so curious, so every time she was on the phone, I would pay attention. And I finally realized she was talking to her *boyfriend.*"

Brent's shoulders tensed up. Victoria had known about the affair. He closed his eyes for a second, his head, his gut, feeling hollow. How could he have been so clueless about what had been happening in his own house when his kid sister knew?

"I was in such shock," Victoria continued. "And then one night I heard her whispering on the phone and crying. She was saying she was 'nervous about the plan.' I had no idea what she meant."

The plan to run away, Brent knew. He pictured his sister, just twelve, standing shell-shocked just beyond a doorway, quiet as a mouse as her mother broke down on the phone.

Victoria was quiet for a few seconds, as if lost in memory. "Then Mom said something about money, that she 'had it' and 'now they could run away together.' I was so stunned. And panicked. I can remember shaking and then running off, trying to unhear what she'd said."

"Oh, Vick," he said, reaching for her hand.

She took in a breath and seemed to be trying to get a hold of herself. "The next day, I tore her room apart looking for that money. I found it in a drawer of her vanity, stuffed inside a cosmetics bag. I just kept thinking of how she was crying, saying she was nervous. I thought if she didn't have the money, she couldn't run away with that man."

Brent felt such a burst of anger at his mother for putting their young daughter in this position. Carrying on an affair that apparently the whole town was whispering about—even if they didn't know who the man was. Talking on the phone in the family home where Victoria had overheard. How could June Woodson have been so careless? Thoughtless?

Because she'd been desperate, Brent knew, his heart half going out to his mother, half aching for what her actions had wrought. His mom had felt trapped in a miserable marriage, and her rekindled romance with her first love had felt like the answer. But she'd stolen. And she was going to run away, then try to get custody of her kids. Barrett had been right that the whole thing was a mess—a terrible mess with so many components.

He stared at his sister, trying to focus. "So you hid the wad of cash. Under that boulder."

Victoria nodded. "And then that night, I heard Mom and Dad arguing. He told her he overheard her talking to her 'lover' on the phone and that he was going to fix it so she couldn't run off on us. Mom was crying. And I got so scared I ran into my room—I was *trembling*. Next thing I heard, the Deroys were gone. A rumor was going around saying that Barrett Jr. had stolen the money. I felt so bad because I knew it was a lie. I typed up a note——*You have the wrong man*—and I put it with the money. And then I tried very hard to forget it."

Her words echoed in his head. "So Mom always must have believed Dad had hidden the money. And Dad thought Mom did. That checks."

Victoria nodded. "And as the years went on, I think I repressed it all, Brent. And then six months ago, when the money and note were found, I just froze up. I'm so sorry." She burst into tears.

Brent stood and walked over to his sister, taking her hands and pulling her up. He wrapped her in a hug, letting her cry. "You were twelve, Vick. And six months ago, when the money was found, I understand why you didn't tell anyone you'd found it and hidden it there. There was little point by then. Barrett's name was cleared. Everyone knew Mom stole the money."

"Brent, you don't have to defend me. I was wrong then and I was wrong six months ago. I accept that. And I want to make it right."

He felt himself stiffen. "How?"

"By going to Mayor Garrett and confessing what I did. I might not have stolen the money, but I knew who really did—and where the money was. And I remained silent. I let someone else be blamed for years. I'll take whatever consequences there are."

He closed his eyes for a second. "That's what you want to do?"

She nodded. "It's what I *have* to do."

He was proud of her. Damned proud. "Well, you're not going to see Mayor Garrett alone." He paced the kitchen for a few seconds, then turned back to his sister. "It's time for an emergency family meeting. Because we're *all* going with you."

Her eyes widened. "You mean Mom and Dad too?"

He nodded.

He was worried for Victoria. But he knew the four of them needed to present themselves to the mayor, possibly to the police as well. Perhaps he'd ask Jenni-Lynn to call in the chief to be there in her office when they all trooped over.

He didn't have to think long and hard about all this to know Victoria was making the right decision. That he was making the right decision to call his family together. The truth was everything.

"Brent?" Victoria said. "You'll get back together with Sage, right? I mean, of all the things that might happen, that's the one assurance I want."

His heart lurched. "I don't know. I feel like something…irrevocably broke there."

Victoria's eyes widened. "*What?* All she did was tell you the truth. Because she didn't want secrets between you."

He'd just thought to himself that the truth was everything. But…

But things had changed between him and Sage during that talk in front of his fireplace. No—not between them. *Inside* him. The wall he'd built up around himself six months ago was back; he could *feel* it. Their romance had started blasting through it, but now it was more fortified than ever.

Even if he wanted to let her in, he didn't think he *could*.

"I'm so sad you're leaving Cheyenne," Sage's good friend Jodie said from where she sat on Sage's bed. Her bestie since sophomore year of high school, Jodie had come over to the ranch to help her pack. With her long, wild auburn curls and round silver eyeglasses, her friend hadn't changed in the fifteen years they'd known each other.

"I'll miss it here," Sage said, standing in front of her open closet and creating *keep* and *donate* piles. "And you, of course."

"So you do you think you'll move to Tenacity, after all?" Jodie asked, putting a stack of sweaters into Sage's big suitcase. Jodie knew all about Brent—then and now. Sage hadn't told her any details about the situation with Victoria Woodson, just that some family issues had come between them. "Or will you go somewhere else? Bozeman has a vibrant arts scene. If you want a smaller city, Kalispell and Whitefish too."

Sage had thought today's long drive from Tenacity to Cheyenne would have given her some clarity. Now that she and her mom had a brand-new relationship, living in Tenacity was first choice. Sage might have moved to Cheyenne when she was still in high school, but she'd always consider Tenacity her home town. And with the dinosaur park and fossil dig all but assured to happen, she was excited about what was to come.

But could she settle down in such a small town when the man she loved—and lost—was right there? When she'd run into him in town, whether in the Silver Spur for coffee or walking through the park? In the short time she'd been in Tenacity, so many places had reminded her of Brent and their first go-round at romance. Now she'd meet friends at Grizzly's or Castillo's, and would remember their dates there. She'd pass the Social Club and envision the two of them line dancing during teen time. She'd pass the road to his ranch and recall their winter picnic...and indoor activities. She'd constantly be a weepy, achy mess.

So she wasn't sure where she was headed. "I just don't know. I want to live in Tenacity. Put down roots there. But..."

Jodie placed a stack of jeans in the suitcase. "I think you should move back, Sage."

Sage added some *donate* items to the big black trash bag and closed it up. "You do? And walk around with a broken heart for all time?"

"I'm just not sure you two are done," Jodie said. "Sounds to me like Brent got caught very off guard with news that was hard to hear, and he reacted."

"He was *really* upset. And he made it clear he never wants to see me again. He asked me to leave his home. And he didn't take my call or respond to my text. That was last night. I haven't heard from all day today either."

"Maybe he just needs some time," Jodie said.

Sage paused with a dress she'd removed from its hanger. "Even so, let's say he forgives me. Let's say he hears that what I said was true." She had to keep things vague; it would be easier to just tell Jodie everything, but Sage couldn't do that. What she knew about Victoria had to be kept private. "He'll still associate me with this ugly story that started fifteen years ago. I think that no matter what, he'll think I took something from him—*peace*."

"Oh, Sage, this whole thing is such a hot mess. From what you've told me, all you did was tell Brent a hard truth to hear. That's not your fault. And the breakup isn't fair. You and Brent belong together."

Sage's heart lurched. She thought so too.

But she knew there was no going back, no going forward.

Chapter Fourteen

In the morning, the sight of his parents and sister sitting in the living room of the Woodson home was more emotional for Brent than he'd expected. For better or worse, this was his family.

Victoria had wanted them both to sleep on everything that had come out, and Brent had agreed that was a good idea. So last night, after Victoria had gone home, he'd called his parents—his mom at the house and his dad at the inn—and asked them to meet him and Victoria at home today at 9:00 a.m. His mother had been upset at the idea of "that man" coming back even for an hour. His father had sounded nervous and wanted to know what the get-together was about. He'd told them he and Victoria would explain all in the morning, and they'd promised to be there.

Now his parents were sitting at opposite ends of the sofa. He and Victoria were on the two high-backed chairs facing them. Brent had brought coffee the way everyone liked it and baked goods from the Silver Spur, which were spread out on the coffee table between them. Cliff Woodson, looking haggard and upset but dressed in his usual khakis and button-down shirt under a fleece vest, was biting into a scone as if he had no issue with his appetite. June Woodson, chin lifted, looking a bit worried, was just holding her steaming coffee. And Victoria had gotten up and was pacing.

"Honey, what's wrong? What's going on?" June asked her daughter. "What's this about?"

Victoria took a deep breath and sat down. Then she launched into the whole story—the one she'd told Brent last night.

"Oh, Vicky," June said, her hand flying to her heart, her expression horrified. Tears sprang to her eyes. "I'm so sorry."

"It was a long time ago," Victoria said. "We've all paid a price for what happened back then. But I had an opportunity to clear Barrett Jr.'s name and I didn't. I had a chance to return the money to the town and I didn't. I need to face the consequences for that."

Clifford stood up, his face red. "Now, hold on here! You were just a little girl!"

"I can excuse my behavior fifteen years ago," Victoria said. "But six months ago. I remained silent."

June sipped her coffee and set it back down. "Honey, there was no point for you to say anything six months ago—and the family that bought the house returned the money to the town."

"That's right," Clifford said, then frowned and turned to Victoria and Brent. He narrowed his eyes at them. "What's going on?" he demanded. "What is this meeting really for?"

"Restitution," Victoria said. "Making things right. For all of us. It's past the statute of limitation for anything that happened back then. But I want the four us to meet with Mayor Garrett and the sheriff and each discuss our parts in what happened fifteen years ago— and six months ago. If anyone has anything to add, I want it stated, *Dad*."

Clifford narrowed his eyes. "What am I being of accused of now?"

"Did you help Marty and Mayor Garrett's husband tamper with the ballots that got Marty elected?" Brent asked. "Tell the truth."

"It's ancient history!" Clifford bellowed.

"Dad, if you want a relationship with Victoria and me," Brent said, "you have to become a better person. That means taking personal responsibility for wrong-doing."

"You two will spend time with me?" Clifford asked, his face softening.

"We can try to build a new relationship as these new people we are," Victoria said. "The better people we'll become. But only if you tell the truth. And only if you vow to do right by us and yourself and this town from here on in."

His father took a deep breath. "I gave Marty and Garrett *advice* for how they might, uh, win the election—meaning who to kiss up to. But that's *it*. I didn't physically do anything. That's the God's honest truth. It's why there wasn't anything linking me to all that."

Brent nodded. "Okay. So you'll prove this by handing over your phone to the chief of police so that they can check your text messages during that time frame?

And so they can turn it over to the prosecutor as well, for evidence, if necessary?"

Clifford brightened. "Yes—and you can have possession of my phone right now so you'll know I couldn't delete anything between now and the meeting." Brent stared at his father, surprised but hopeful. He had a feeling, finally, that Clifford was telling the truth. His dad hung his head. "I've lost everything, including the respect of my children. And I want that back. I know I have a lot of work to do to change how you two see me. But I promise I'll work very hard on that."

Brent eyed Victoria, who had tears in her eyes. She nodded at their father, whose entire body deflated with relief. Brent held out his hand for the phone, which Clifford gave him. He also nodded at his dad and gave him a half-hearted clap on the shoulder. A small sign that Brent was open to possibilities.

He turned to his mother. "Mom? Are you willing to tell your story from start to finish to Mayor Garrett and the chief of police? So that both Vick and I hear it from you?"

Tears filled June Woodson's eyes. "Yes. I'd do anything to have a second chance at being a family. With the two of you," she said pointedly, refusing to even look at her husband.

Clifford narrowed his gaze at his wife, but then the fight seemed to go out of him. "I was never a good husband to you, Juney. I knew I was second choice when Barrett Sr. left town when we were teens. I guess I always resented you for still being in love with him when you married me."

"I did love you, Cliff. But we're getting divorced. We can each have good relationships with our children. But our family will be very different. Maybe one day, we can even be civil to each other," she added.

"That would be nice," Clifford said without an ounce of sarcasm.

"There are two more things," Brent said. "I think that all four us should volunteer once a week for the next year at least in whatever capacity JenniLynn sees fits. It's a way to give back to Tenacity."

Three heads nodded. And Victoria looked relieved.

"And finally, I want the four of us to sit down with the Deroy family—and for each of us to apologize." He turned to his mom. "I know emotionally that may be hard on you, to sit at the same table with—" Brent let the rest go; they all knew what Brent meant. "But Barrett deserves that."

Three heads nodded.

"Good," Brent said. "I'll set it up with Barrett."

They were all quiet for a moment, everything registering.

"Will Vicky get in any trouble?" June asked, her face full of worry.

"I don't think so," Brent said. "It's an acknowledgment. An apology. A promise to help the town. And then we can all move on."

"I'll do whatever I need to," Clifford said. "But I'll deal with that. I want my kids to think highly of me again." Tears came to his eyes, and Brent could not have been more surprised.

Victoria held up her coffee. "To family. And Tenacity," she said.

They all held up their cups and took a sip.

And for the first time in months, Brent felt something ease inside him, as if he truly believed a better
future was possible for the Woodsons.

But he was putting his past and everything associ-
ated with this terrible tale behind him. And that closed
the door on Sage too.

That night, Brent was slipping his horse some carrot
slices in the barn, his mind a jumble of all that had gone
on that day, when he heard a car pulling up. He zipped
his bomber jacket and went to see who was there. At
this point, it could be anyone. A member of his family. Mayor Garrett. The chief of police.

The four Woodsons had indeed gone to JenniLynn's
office with their plan to make restitution, to further
apologize, and then they'd all been so spent that they'd
each gone their separate ways. Brent might not have
stolen money from the town, or blackmailed a family or
have known the truth the whole time and remained silent, but he'd been guilty of being self-absorbed, cocky,
and only out for himself. If he'd been a different person, he'd have noticed his beloved sister, who'd always
been so important to him, was struggling. Instead, he
was hanging out with his pack, none of whom he'd call
friends anymore. But Brent had become a different man
these past six months, and this new truth about Victoria had changed him even more.

What it had told him was that he still had work to do.

Victoria had to have been a nervous wreck that her part in the truth would come out. Had he noticed? He'd just chalked up her keeping to herself to the wretched news about his parents, and focused on how the fallout had affected him. But she'd been hiding a big secret. And had the *supposedly* new Brent Woodson noticed? No.

One more thing he'd vowed to do as part of his own restitution was to give back in other ways. Volunteering. Being more aware of neighbors who needed help, whether financially or because of medical conditions. Caring about people—and not just as far as his own reputation was concerned.

He'd left that meeting with his chin up, in a good place. His parents—and more importantly, his sister—would not face any charges due to the statute of limitations. And since there was simply no proof that his father had committed election interference, Clifford Woodson would not be in trouble. Brent had handed over his father's phone for the police chief to read Cliff's text messages during that time-frame, and except for a flurry of texts to Marty about how to *win* the election and who to kiss up to in order to *potentially* secure their vote, there was nothing remotely criminal. Brent didn't wish prison on his father, but he sure was getting away with a lot. Then again, Cliff had lost just about everything he'd once cared about.

His father had been so relieved that he'd surprised everyone in the mayor's office by offering to volunteer *twice* a week for the town for the next five years. Brent knew that Jennilynn wouldn't let Cliff anywhere near the town hall, so he just might see his dad collecting trash from the park with a litter-picker and trash bag over his shoulder. It was a start.

Brent would engineer the meeting of the Woodson and Deroy families for the apology. He'd already reached out to Barrett about the idea, and his friend had immediately replied that he thought it was a good idea and he'd discuss it with his folks.

So who'd come to talk some more? Given how well the meeting had gone, how receptive and warm the mayor and chief had been, he'd welcome anyone to further discuss what had been talked about. The headlights on the approaching vehicle made it impossible to see until whoever it was parked.

Ah, it was Barrett Deroy. He was again wearing the cowboy hat Brent had given him. Brent stepped outside to meet him.

"It's cold out tonight," Barrett said as he approached. "Talk in the house?"

"Sure," Brent said, and they headed inside. "Something to drink?"

"I have a craving for eggnog, actually. Got any left over from Christmas?"

Brent laughed. "Nope. I hate eggnog. How about a ginger ale?"

"Next-best thing," Barrett said.

With their drinks, they sat down in the living room. "What's up?" Brent asked. "Everything okay with the foundation?" Had word spread about Victoria's involvement with the stolen money and investors dropped out? There'd been no request from the family to keep that quiet; that went against the very point. Brent wouldn't tell Barrett about it, though; that was either the mayor's or Victoria's place.

"I got a call from JenniLynn earlier," he said. "A call that did my heart some good. She said she met with the town council, and Tenacity would like to use some of the money that was returned from the theft to the revitalization efforts since a large part had always been earmarked for that in the first place. So we're now *past* the figure we were after to officially make the park a go. The dinosaur park *will* happen."

He was glad Barrett knew. *Phew.* Brent smiled, his heart cracking wide open. "That's very good news."

"It was a busy day and I couldn't get away until now, but I wanted to come thank you in person. I know you must have had something to do with getting your entire family to march down to the mayor's office with the chief of police there. And the apology is a good way to put this whole thing behind us."

Brent couldn't be more relieved—and grateful that Barrett Deroy was such an amazing human being. "I think the Woodsons are at a good starting point for doing just that. My parents will be finalizing their divorce, but Vick and I will be seeing them more regularly, if separately. There won't be Sunday dinners, but a deep rift has started filling in some."

"Good. Your sister came to see me today after I talked to JenniLynn," Barrett said, and Brent wasn't surprised. He'd had a feeling she'd do that. "She wanted to apologize to me right away for not speaking up. And she told me how you found out her secret about hiding the money."

Brent turned away, looking out the window at the dark sky. "So I guess you know that Sage and I broke up."

"I just don't know *why*. Didn't you see my note? You're not supposed to give up on love, Woodson."

Brent looked at his friend, whose disappointment was clear. "To be honest, Barrett, I've tried to emulate you the past six months. To not be bitter. To let people think what they will and to just be myself. But you have this way of letting go that I don't have."

"Not letting go could have cost me Nina," Barrett said. "Being stubborn, holding onto the past, being my own worst enemy. And for what? To lose the best thing that ever happened to me? If you want to emulate me, Brent, go get that woman."

Brent felt a pinch in the region of his heart. He missed Sage so badly. But he'd screwed up. He shook his head and got up, walking to the windows to stare out.

"What's the *real* story?" Barrett asked. "It makes no sense that you're upset at Sage for telling you what turned out to be true—*and* ended up starting your family on a healing path. Why would you cut her out of your life?"

Brent had been asking himself that same question since yesterday. He'd never been able to understand—until now. Until his *own* truth knocked him over the head. He turned back to Barrett. "She feels like part of my past that I'm ashamed of," Brent admitted, almost unable to believe he'd actually said it. "Do you know what I mean?" His voice sounded faraway to him. "I didn't deserve her fifteen years ago, and I don't deserve her now. She came to me with the truth, and I told her I didn't believe her, that she was wrong. I told her to leave my house. I want to put the past behind me—and she's part of that past."

"No. She's your *future*, Brent. And you can rectify what happened with Sage. Just like you did with your family and the town."

He let out a hard breath. "It's not as simple as an apology and returning money with interest."

"Actually, it's simpler. Just an apology will do. And an admission."

"Of what?" Brent asked.

"Of *love*, dummy. That you love her. That you were wrong. That you'll spend the rest of your life making up for almost losing her for good."

Talk about a truth knocking him upside the head. He *did* love Sage Abernathy. Very much.

"What if I blew it, though? What if she won't talk to me? I heard she left town and went back to Cheyenne. She's done with me." His chest seized up and he dropped back down on the sofa.

"If she left town, she's back."

Hope flared. "What? Your saw her in town today?"

Barrett nodded with a smile. "On my way here—I saw her little car parked by the Tenacity Inn."

Brent stood up. "No offense but I have somewhere to be."

"Yeah, you do," Barrett said. "Go get her."

Chapter Fifteen

Sage was sitting at the desk in her room at the Tenacity Inn, scrolling through homes for sale in town. There were several, from ranches on the outskirts to a few small capes close to town. Sage couldn't quite see herself in any of them.

She knew why too.

Because she only saw herself at Brent's ranch. Waking up every morning in that sun-drenched bedroom beside him. Sitting on the back deck in chaises and watching the sunrise. Walking to the barn to bring the man she loved a thermos of coffee while he worked. Painting the landscape. Painting *him*.

A life there with the man she loved.

Despite her heavy heart and how much thinking about Brent hurt, she wasn't running from the town she wanted to call home. Sage was done with living in the shadows. She was now a person who spoke up in all regards. And a very loud voice inside her was shouting for her to put down roots in Tenacity. If she ran into Brent in town, she'd let herself feel that hurt, let herself ache, and slowly, she'd lose herself in her art until her heart started to heal. If it ever would.

She'd fallen hard for Brent Woodson. Getting over him wouldn't come easy.

The phone on the desk rang, and she grabbed the receiver. Why would the front desk be calling her? "Hello?"

"Ms. Abernathy, there's someone here to see you. Brent Woodson. Shall I give him your room number?"

Sage gasped. Brent was here? "Yes, send him up, and thank you."

She moved to the door, her heart pounding out of her chest. Had he come to say he was sorry for how things had ended but it was for the best?

When he knocked, she pulled open the door, and the sight of him brought both joy and tears to her eyes. He looked so serious, so handsome. So… Brent. How she'd missed him.

"I knew you left town—small-town gossip," he said. "But then *thanks* to small-town gossip, I heard you were back. I forgot you wouldn't be in the same room and actually knocked on your old door. A man answered and I almost died."

Sage's eyes widened. "Um, I wouldn't have moved on *that* fast, Brent."

"I know. I was so in my head about whether or not you'd ever forgive me that seeing him caught me by surprise. I quickly realized you were given a new room."

She offered him a wobbly smile, still stuck on what he'd said about forgiving him. Was he here for only that? To say he was sorry and then leave?

"Come on in," she said, trying not to be too hopeful. Brent was both complicated and not at all. And she was very good at reading him. But right now, she didn't know *what* to expect.

He stepped inside, the man she loved so much, in his familiar black leather bomber jacket, his favorite plaid scarf at his neck, and his Stetson covering his blond hair. All she wanted right now was to grab him in her arms and hug him hard. And never let him go.

"First, about that apology," he said. "Even if you'd been wrong about my sister hiding the money, I would still owe you that. I handled that last talk badly, Sage. And I'm very sorry. I should have known you had my best interests at heart. *Our* best interests."

She tilted her head. "You spoke to Victoria about it?"

He nodded and launched into quite a story that had her gasping more than once and sitting down on the edge of the bed to process everything. Victoria's admission. The entire Woodson family meeting with the mayor and police chief. Victoria going to apologize to Barrett for not speaking up. The two families meeting for the Woodsons' apologies.

"Thanks to you, Sage, everything came out. The final pieces of the puzzle. And even though my parents are divorcing, our family is stronger than ever. Because there are no secrets anymore. Everyone is now able to move on—in their way."

Her hand flew to her heart. "I'm so happy to hear that. Wow."

"I don't know if you can forgive me for how I acted," he said. "It was easier for me to be mad at you than accept the truth. Because I wasn't done growing the hell up. But thanks to you, I had to really look at myself again. I'm so sorry, Sage."

She stood and walked over to him, taking both his hands in hers. "I fully accept your apology. And I'm sorry for keeping secrets from you, Brent. I hope you can forgive *me*."

His expression so serious, he looked down at their entwined hands. "Of course I can. And do."

"Good," she said. "Is that why you came? To apologize?"

"That first, but I have a lot more to say."

Hope flared inside her. "I'm listening."

He sat beside her. "I'd been so focused on myself that I never let anyone in before. And I realized—with a little help tonight from Barrett Deroy—that I was still trying to keep you out. Because loving you meant really exposing myself. Everything I am. If you'll have me, Sage, I promise you that I'll always listen, always hear you, always trust you."

She wrapped her arms around his neck. "Oh, I'll have you."

He smiled and kissed her, then pulled her against him. "Thank you for forgiving me. For giving me a *third* chance."

"Third time is always the charm," she said.

Brent kissed her again and held her close. She could feel his love for her vibrating in his body. "And guess what? Turns out that the foundation has enough to go ahead with the dinosaur park."

"And you'll have some cushion, then. Because not only are my parents investing, but I am too. I'm going to use some of my small trust fund for Tenacity's future."

He smiled, his blue eyes sparkling. "Our *children's* future. Just think—they'll be running around the dinosaur park, *ooh*ing and *ahh*ing at the exhibits and fossils."

Sage was so happy she could burst. "Our kids?" He was kind of getting ahead of himself there, but that was more than fine with her. "How many are we having?"

"As many as you want," he said.

"Five?"

He grinned. "Done. Oh wait—I was so busy apologizing I almost forgot a good first step between right now and our five kids."

She tilted her head. "What do you mean?"

Brent got down on one knee. "If the jewelry store had been open, I would have charged in and bought you a ring I know you'd love. And I'd propose with that. I'll be hitting the shop first thing tomorrow morning. But in the meantime…"

Tears of joy filled Sage's eyes and she blinked them back. She didn't want to miss a moment of this by sobbing.

"Sage Abernathy, will you do me the honor of marrying me?"

She looked at the man she loved with all her heart. "Yes. I absolutely will."

He stood and scooped her up in his arms, twirling them both around. Then he kissed her so tenderly, with such emotion, that the tears were back.

"I love you so much, Brent Woodson."

"I love you, too, Sage. And I'll spend the rest of my days showing you how much. That's a promise." He hugged her, resting his head atop hers. Then he pulled back and looked at her. "So what's this about your parents' investing? They came around?"

She nodded. "My dad worked a little magic on my mom about letting me live my own life. And it helped them both understand that if *I* trust you, *they* trust you. For the first time in my life, I know what it's like to feel like my mother is my friend."

"I'm so happy for you. And it's a good thing the Woodsons are going to be civil to each other, because they'll have an engagement party to attend."

"I'm so excited for everything to come," she said. "I'm going to have a sister-in-law!"

He grinned. "I think Victoria is going to be very happy to welcome you to the family." He gave her one more kiss and ran a hand down her long, blond hair. "What do you say we check you out of this place, and you come home—to the ranch. *Our* ranch. You'll have to decide where you want to set up your art studio. Or I can build you a new one on the property—facing the mountains. Anything you want, Sage."

She was so moved, so deeply touched, that she couldn't speak for a moment. "This has been some do-over, Brent."

With that, Sage packed up for the third time in a short period and left the inn hand in hand with her fiancé, ready for their future to begin right now. She was going *home*.

Epilogue

It was a beautiful day for winter in Montana. The sun was shining. The temperature was an almost balmy forty-seven degrees. And once again, it seemed the entire town had come out to celebrate.

The last time Brent had been in a big crowd like this was for JenniLynn Garrett's swearing-in ceremony in the park. Now, in a huge field not far from where the dinosaur bones had been found, a ribbon-cutting ceremony would formally declare this as the site of the future Tenacity Dinosaur Park.

And like at the inauguration, Brent stood on the makeshift stage—which his father had arranged for—near the borrowed podium. Mayor Garrett was speaking into the microphone about how the groundbreaking for the park would have to wait till spring, when the frozen earth would make digging for fossils easier. But thanks to their new investors, they were going to be able to start construction very soon on the Tenacity Dinosaur Center. There were claps and cheers. Beside Brent stood Barrett Deroy and Seth Taylor. They'd all be speaking about the plans for the park, and giving their thanks for all the investors, from five dollar donations to tens of thousands. Even little kids had donated their piggy banks. That had brought tears to Brent's eyes.

Beside Brent was his beautiful fiancée, Sage. Beside Barrett was his fiancée, Nina Sanchez. And beside Seth was his love, Andrea Spence, the paleontologist who'd be working closely on the dig for more dinosaur bones. There was a lot of love on this stage.

And Barrett had been right. Real love *was* hard to come by. Now that Brent had found that someone he could trust, he'd never let her go.

He gave his fiancée's hand a squeeze, so grateful for her. She smiled at him, and he felt his heart fill. As Brent looked out into the crowd, he could see all their families, the Woodsons, the Abernathys, the Deroys, the Sanchezes, and the Taylors.

As his gaze landed on Victoria, she burst into a smile and waved at him, and he waved back. Beside Victoria was her best friend Cassie Trent and her fiancé, Graham Callahan. He spotted Seth's brother's fiancé's sister—quite a mouthful—Maggie Cooper and her fiancé Braden Parker with their kids, Cody and Delilah. And there were Shane Corey and Remi Hawkins in their Stetsons, arms around each other. And pregnant Winter Sanchez with her husband, Luca, his hand resting on her baby bump. Brent thought about what he and Sage had talked about in her hotel room the day they'd gotten engaged. Kids. Five of them. The idea made him grin. Bring it on.

Missing were Brent's parents and Barrett's folks. After the relatively short and somewhat awkward meeting between the two families a few days ago, the Woodsons' heartfelt apologies and the Deroys' kind acceptance, the group had dispersed, everyone feeling relieved. Brent knew his parents would be keeping a low profile in town, but perhaps in time, with their efforts at becoming better people, Clifford and June would find their way in the community.

As Mayor Garrett announced that Andrea Spence was the director of the dinosaur park, the crowd burst into applause. Even though Tenacity would have to wait a few months to start digging for fossils, come spring they'd be in the path of a full lunar eclipse. Tenacity would be celebrating that as a part of the campaign to "Illuminate Tenacity" to generate extra interest in town as folks near and far awaited the dig to commence.

Brent turned to his fiancée, whose diamond engagement ring twinkled in the bright sunshine. The future was indeed already bright for them—and for all of Tenacity.

* * * * *

Don't miss
My Heart Belongs to the Maverick
by Carrie Nichols
the first installment in
Montana Mavericks: Legacy of Tenacity

Catch up with the previous installments in the series
Montana Mavericks: Behind Closed Doors

The Maverick's Dating Deal
by New York Times *bestselling author*
Christine Rimmer

The Maverick's Forever Home
by USA TODAY *bestselling author Sasha Summers*

Lassoed by a Maverick
by Rochelle Alers

Snowed in with the Maverick
by Elle Douglas

The Maverick's Mistletoe Bride
by Brenda Harlen

Available now!

Get up to 4 Free Books!

We'll send you 2 free books from each series you try
PLUS a free Mystery Gift.

FREE Value Over **$25**

Both the **Harlequin® Special Edition** and **Harlequin® Heartwarming™** series feature compelling novels filled with stories of love and strength where the bonds of friendship, family and community unite.